"I've often wondered," Max said, "what I'd be like as a father. I think I might be rather good."

Often wondered? How cruel could life be? Laura wanted to yell. Why hadn't he wanted to be a father five years ago? Why hadn't he wanted a family as much as he clearly did now? And why did he have to keep shoving his happy daddy act in her face all the time? Maybe if he knew what had happened to her he'd choose his words more carefully and stop breaking her heart. But she couldn't bring herself to tell him.

Max appeared at her side. "Cheers," he said, handing her a glass of wine.

"What could we possibly be cheering about?" Laura muttered, taking a huge gulp.

"Our good fortune!"

"*This* is good fortune? A miserable little cottage, a ferocious gale and stair-rods of rain outside, two strange children and—and..." Her voice wobbled, betraying her pent-up emotions. "And...worst of...all, *you!*"

Childhood in Portsmouth, England, meant grubby knees, flying pigtails and happiness for *SARA WOOD*. Poverty drove her from typist and seaside landlady to teacher, till writing finally gave her the freedom her Romany blood craved. Happily married, she has two handsome sons: Richard is calm, dependable, drives tankers; Simon is a roamer—silversmith, roofer, welder, always with beautiful girls. Sara lives in the Cornish countryside. Her glamorous writing life alternates with her passion for gardening, which allows her to be carefree and grubby again!

Sara Wood gives us
"a passionate conflict and smoldering sensuality."
—*Romantic Times*

SARA WOOD

Temporary Parents

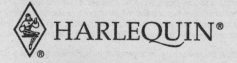

HARLEQUIN®

TORONTO • NEW YORK • LONDON
AMSTERDAM • PARIS • SYDNEY • HAMBURG
STOCKHOLM • ATHENS • TOKYO • MILAN • MADRID
PRAGUE • WARSAW • BUDAPEST • AUCKLAND

For Anna and Chris at Headlands Hotel,
and for The Girls.

ISBN 0-373-11974-7

TEMPORARY PARENTS

First North American Publication 1998.

CHAPTER ONE

THE trilling of the phone ripped into Laura's unconsciousness. Her hand fumbled about, knocking over the bedside lamp, two paperbacks, a china hedgehog and a mug with its dregs of hot chocolate before connecting with the receiver.

''Lo?' she mumbled, drowsily trying to right everything and getting a chocolatey hand for her pains.

'Laura?'

She sat bolt-upright in bed, suddenly startled and alert. 'Yes, Max?' she squeaked.

It was an unmistakable, honey-on-steel version of her name. *L-a-u-r-a*. Shivers went down her back. Her hand pressed against her chest, as if that would stop the acrobatics of her heart. Max. The years rolled back...

'I'm coming to see you.'

She blinked. It was pitch-dark in her small bedsit. She pushed back the flopping mass of unruly black hair which could have been obscuring her view—but it was *still* dark. When she checked the luminous dial of her clock, her huge, summer-sky-coloured eyes rounded in complete amazement.

'At four in the morning? Oh, for heaven's sake!'

She slammed the phone down and hauled the duvet over her head. She had to get up in an hour! Angrily she listened to the muted, persistent ringing, wishing that she'd yanked the whole thing from its socket.

And then as she lay there, hating Max, wishing he'd give up, she finally put two and two together. There could be only one reason Max wanted to see her: the secret she and her older sister Fay had kept to themselves for the past five years.

Laura sat up again in horror. Perhaps he knew the truth now. What would he do? Tell Daniel, Fay's husband? Then what?

She shuddered, suddenly icy cold. Flinging back the duvet, she launched herself in panic at the phone. Both of them landed on the floor, and her African Grey parrot woke up and started screeching in alarm.

'Shut up, Fred...! Oh, this wretched thing...!' she wailed in frustration, trying to untangle the cord from her ankle.

She could hear Max shouting somewhere in the depths of the receiver and felt vindictively sorry that the crash hadn't burst his eardrums.

'Yes? What?' she demanded, cross and out of breath.

'What the hell's going on? Who's there with you?' Max yelled, sounding agitated. Fred screamed on relentlessly.

'It's all right, darling!' she crooned, anxious for her beloved, neurotic pet's state of mind. 'Coo-coo-coo—'

'What?'

'I was speaking to my parrot!' she snapped, feeling hysterical.

Fred's screeching was drilling through her head. She fumbled for the light switch on the fallen lamp and switched it on.

'A parrot.'

Stung by Max's slicing tone, she clenched her teeth and tried to ignore the implication that he was dealing with a fool. Max could sneer for England.

'Hang on!' she cried, wincing as Fred's screeches scythed through her. 'I've got to calm him down. He's emotionally disturbed.'

'For pity's sake—!'

Cutting him off in mid-curse, she scrambled unsteadily to her feet, thinking that now she was emotionally disturbed too. Dammit, why had Max crawled out of the woodwork?

Gently she removed the cover on Fred's night cage, murmuring to him a few soothing words. How nice, she thought wistfully, if someone could do that for her.

The mollified Fred tucked his denuded head under his wing and she stroked him fondly. She'd rescued him from an animal shelter where she worked on weekends, smitten by the ugly, bald, mangy looking bird...and wanting something to love.

Her heart contracted. With her dark, Celtic brows zapped together in a fierce scowl, she stared miserably at the phone, unwilling to make contact with Max. She'd got over him. But not the consequences of their affair.

Max had got her pregnant five years ago, when she had been eighteen and he had been twenty-four. Then he'd moved back to a fiancée he'd had stashed away in Surrey. Then, in a matter of weeks, on to Laura's sister. Then, who knows? One, two, three. Bunny-hopping through women with a staggering nonchalance.

To Laura's fury, her eyes filled with tears. She'd thought she'd put all that pain behind her. And now Max was dragging unwanted memories back to the forefront of her mind.

Her small, dainty hands fluttered in a bewildered gesture at her stupidity. She knew how and why she'd got pregnant, why she'd taken that mad and fatal risk. They had held back for a long time and he had been leaving for France... And she'd loved him so utterly that when he'd started touching her she hadn't ever wanted him to stop and had driven him beyond the point of return.

That one occasion had been enough for her to conceive.

Carefully she replaced Fred's cover. Like it or not, she had to see Max. She must know his intentions.

Trembling, and afraid of facing the past, she resumed her position on the floor, needing something good and solid beneath her shaking body. She took a deep breath, and spoke before she could chicken out.

'I'm listening now.'

'Good. I'll be arriving at one o'clock lunchtime. Be there. It's important.'

'Be where?' she asked guardedly, hating his curtness and the way her voice quaked.

'The baker's shop. Where you work—'

'How do you know this?' she cried in alarm.

'I've been talking to Daniel.'

Laura's right hand wobbled so much that she had to support it with her left. 'Oh.'

Dimly she heard him trying to get her attention. She couldn't speak. Her whole body felt completely paralysed. He could already have told Daniel! Fay's marriage and the future of Fay's two children could be in real danger with Max around. He could ruin Fay's life. Laura closed her eyes. As he'd ruined *hers*.

When she'd learnt of Max's affair with her own sister, she'd been in the fifth month of her pregnancy. The news had shocked her so deeply that she hadn't been able to eat. Some time—she didn't know when—her baby had stopped moving.

She felt the scream building up inside her, fighting for release. Her baby. Dead.

Of course she'd willed it to live. Refused to believe that Max's child—her only link with him—had been lost.

She'd waited, day after day, sure that her baby would wake, punch her with its little fists, kick her with its tiny feet…

She blanched. Her stomach cramped. All those hope-ridden days of carrying her dead baby. Then the

high fever, the hours of lonely agony until her aunt had
found her, crying with pain in the bathroom.

In her head she could still hear the sound of her rack-
ing sobs when she'd known for sure that Max had
brought about the death of his own child—even though
he hadn't even known of its existence.

For days she'd lain in her hospital bed, weak and
numb, with a nurse in constant attendance. And then...a
sympathetic doctor had appeared. He'd told her that the
infection had meant the removal of her womb and she
could never have children. But it would never show,
he'd said cheerfully, as if that would somehow console
her.

She hunched up in misery. Max's philandering had
taken away from her the one thing she'd longed for, ever
since she could remember.

A happy marriage. Children. A whole row of them in
ascending sizes. Oh, *God*! It was tearing her heart to
shreds...

'Laura!'

But she was weeping too much now to speak—and
was too proud to let him know that. Loathing the very
sound of him, she dropped the receiver onto its cradle.
And then disconnected the phone completely before
flinging herself back into bed.

In the shop below her bedsit, there had been an epidemic
of babies that morning. One set of blonde twins in
matching red rompers and cosy hats to combat the
October weather. A huge bruiser with the sweetest mar-
malade curls. And the endearing Rufus with his lopsided,
windy smile.

Laura gripped the order book tightly. One deep breath.
Another. Slow, steady. Rufus was now safely outside in
his buggy on fashionable Sloane Street, softening up un-
wary strangers with every waft of his incredible lashes.

'Wait till you have one of your own!' his mother had said happily. 'Stretchmarks, sleepless nights, nappies…!'

Sounded wonderful.

But what had Laura done after that innocently tactless remark? Produced a thin smile and hustled for a decision on the Christening cake design. Refused to look at the child again despite the urge to reach out and stroke his peachy cheek…

'That's the second baby you've cut dead!' scolded Luke, emerging from the office.

With a face like stone, she dived under the counter and replaced the order book, hoping against hope that would be the last bundle of joy she saw that day.

Laura made much of checking the ribbons and flat-packed cake boxes. She thought of little Rufus with his mass of black hair, saucer eyes and tiny, screwed-up, dear little face that could have melted steel girders, let alone Laura's susceptible heart.

As she pretended to root about under the counter, she caught herself responding belatedly to him, the gentle curves of her mouth lifting wistfully.

Rot in hell, Max! she thought, and the sweet-sad smile was sharply erased out. This situation would never alter, so she might as well get used to it.

'Will you come out of there?'

Reluctantly she emerged and straightened, realising as she did so that Luke was warming to his theme.

'Look, Laura, in the two weeks you've been here you've not exactly been Mary Poppins as far as kiddies are concerned.' He looked at her curiously and she immediately turned her back and began fiddling with the cakes on the shelf behind. 'What's the matter with you?' he asked in exasperation.

Remain calm. Pretend his imagination has run away with him.

'I don't know what you mean,' she managed, with a fair stab at surprise.

Now take the cake from the shelf. Read the lettering. 'Happy 30th Birthday, Jasper'. Admire your skill in creating a BMW convertible with only Victoria sponge, icing and your talent to play with. Place it in its box for collection and mind the wing mirrors...

'You ignored that baby! I don't know what he ever did to you!'

Luke, the owner of Sinful Cakes and Indecent Puddings, was clearly not going to let the matter rest. Blindly she feigned an interest in the shelf again.

'Don't you realise it's part of your job to coo and sigh and make those noises women make whenever they see babies?'

'Yes. Shall I restack the shelves with sugar mice?' she asked, her strained voice squeaky enough to belong to a terrified mouse itself.

'No!' Luke grabbed her small, rigid shoulders and determinedly turned her around.

She avoided his eyes, too wound up for a confrontation. Two hours, eight minutes to go before Max turned up. The clock had been counting down in her head all morning, with an unbearable tension increasing every second, just as if she were sitting in a command centre and waiting for a missile launch.

Already her mouth was dry, her hands shaking. Something was happening to her lips. They were beginning to tremble—

'Laura...' came Luke's softly spoken concern.

'Oh, please!' she whimpered.

Gentleness was unfair! She could have borne anything but that! She made a half-hearted attempt to twist from beneath his hands but he was too much of a vast and friendly bear to be evaded by a five-foot-two slip of a female on teetering heels.

'Don't,' she pleaded, hopelessly scared of losing control.

He set her free. But she couldn't move. A sense of hopelessness held her in place just as he'd left her, head drooping, body taut.

The door was being bolted. The bell disabled. There was the sound of the 'Open/Closed' notice being turned around. Luke's footsteps coming closer. His hand supporting her elbow.

'Coffee and a chat, I think.'

He had such a warm brown, tender voice, as if he knew something of the trauma she contained so silently. He would make a willing listener, and she liked him enormously.

They cooked together in the bakery, shared the deliveries to swanky parties in Knightsbridge where the shop outlet was based and worked behind the counter as a happy and friendly team.

But she didn't want to tell anyone. If she did, she might break up. That was the last thing she wanted, with Max on his way. She knew Luke would want some kind of explanation, though.

He shut the door which led into the office. There was the delicious smell of baking from the ovens beyond. He moved her bakery sneakers aside and pushed her into an armchair with the obvious intention of settling her down for a confidential heart-to-heart.

'I know something's wrong. You're terrific with customers. You care. People respond to you. But kids are another matter. You clam up. So…what do you have against them?'

'Nothing.' She adored them. That was the trouble.

Her face crumpled and the first sob rushed up from her chest. Then Luke was kneeling beside her, holding her, patting her back, murmuring soothingly into her thick bob of black hair.

'Oh, curses!' She'd wanted to look wonderful when Max turned up. A kind of 'look what you turned down' defiance. To appear independent, successful, content and strong. Instead, she'd be bag-eyed and ready to cry at his first scathing remark. He'd be bound to condemn her and Fay for being push-overs. She'd be pathetic—too feeble to stand up to him.

'Hush, hush,' Luke said, consolingly.

It was a long time later before the unstoppable flood of tears dried up. Luke made her a strong, sweet coffee and then she plucked up courage and gave him a shortened version of her story.

'I—I can't have children, Luke—' There was a considerable pause while she drank long and deep, forcing the coffee past the mass of whatever was trying to block her throat. 'I adore them,' she said in a small, unhappy voice. 'It's as simple as that. And my ex-boyfriend's coming here lunchtime with some dreadful news about my sister.'

She found that she'd been squeezing Luke's hand tightly, and eased her grip, leaving a red mark and the impression of her short nails in his palm.

So much passion in her! Who would ever guess? Laura Tremaine, dull and plain! Pint-sized, snub-nosed, with a skewed, enormous mouth. Overlooked because of her bubbly, beautiful and sexy sister but with a cauldron of emotion simmering beneath an apparently docile surface.

'I think there's much more to that story, but I won't pry,' Luke said shrewdly. 'Go upstairs. Gather yourself together. When Max comes, I'll send him up. I'll be glued to the intercom in case you need me. Go on!' he urged, when she hesitated.

'You're very kind.'

'Selfish,' he corrected. 'You're a damn good cook,

Laura. I don't want to lose you. We'll come to some arrangement about the baby side of things—'

'No. It won't be a problem.' She stood up, feeling a little better for her outburst. 'I'm OK now. Honestly. And...thanks again. You've been very understanding.'

Luke opened the door to the shop and then paused. 'Not surprising. I knew the signs. My wife can't have kids either, you see.'

Laura went quite cold. Slowly her gaze swivelled to meet his and she recognised his sense of loss with immediate empathy. Only people who were denied children could ever know that desperate, almost frantic feeling of need. It was so fierce and uncontrollable that it could ruin the whole of your life and every relationship that ever came your way.

Max had changed her life totally. She was different—who she was, what she did, her friends, everything. Boyfriends had complained she didn't give of herself. True. How could she, when she'd nothing to give ultimately?

She felt that her status as a woman had become flawed and inferior, like faulty goods. A hopeless sensation of inadequacy had grown inside her, swelling up and occupying every thought and action as if she had a phantom pregnancy. She knew she'd never get over it, however deep she tried to bury it. The sadness would stay with her for the rest of her life.

Thanks, Max.

And here was Luke, telling her his most personal secret. She held out her arms in silent sympathy, and Luke walked into them. There was nothing sexual about the gesture for either of them. Just two unhappy people linked by a poignant tragedy.

'Glad I told you,' she said, Luke's soft jacket muffling her words.

'Yup.' He hugged her harder.

At some stage, someone began to bang on the street door. Although Luke's bulk obscured her vision of the impatient customer, Laura realised they must be in full view.

'Bang goes your reputation,' she said, stepping back and producing a wry smile.

It wasn't funny, but Luke laughed, releasing some of the emotional tension between them.

'Sounds like Jasper's come for his BMW! Upstairs now,' he urged. 'Put the slap on. Don't let Max get under your skin. Stick it out. Some time…you might like to meet my wife. You'll like her.'

He gave a sentimental, dreamy smile and Laura wondered if *she* would ever find a man who loved her unconditionally.

'Thanks.'

Laura touched his chest in an affectionate gesture, and ran up the narrow stairs to her bedsit, wishing her legs weren't shaking so much. She was dreading this meeting.

Her arrival was greeted noisily by Fred. Her face softened and she went over to the free-standing perch by the window.

'Hi, Fred, darling!' she murmured, affectionately tickling his stubbly head. He nuzzled up and made ecstatic clicks with his beak. 'Got to dash,' she told him reluctantly, and glanced at her watch.

Laura groaned. A thousand butterflies took off in her stomach and began a pitched battle. It was nearly her lunch hour already! Max would be here at one. He was brutally punctual. Where had the time gone?

She whirled and inspected herself in the dressing-table mirror. She looked awful. Rumpled and crumpled with red-rimmed eyes and a blotchy face—and her hair flicking out in all directions and looking as if she'd spent the morning having it whipped up by the dough mixer.

As for her dress... It wasn't flattering at all. Wondering exactly what was suitable for meeting an ex-lover with a confession to make, she quickly slipped the simple grey jersey down to the floor and stepped out of it, mentally running through the limited choice in her wardrobe.

Something smart. Severe. That would help to keep her nerves together. She was a firm believer that clothes could alter moods.

The shoes were fine. High, as she always liked them, giving her a feeling of authority and efficiency. And altitude. And they bolstered her confidence when dealing with the well-off, well-bred clientele.

Since Max was just on six feet and towered over her, she'd need both confidence and height or he'd be constantly looking down his nose at her. She'd keep them on.

Help! A quarter to one! She felt weak with apprehension. Better hurry. Get the face sorted. The more barriers, the better.

She sped into the bathroom as fast as her smart shoes would allow, feeling chilly in just her chainstore bra, briefs, suspender belt and stockings. Frantically she turned on the cold tap and gasped aloud with shock as she splashed water over her swollen face—and accidentally flung some at her chest, too.

Somewhere in the background, Fred squawked. Probably worried she was being attacked, she thought, absently applying soap to her face. He'd be brilliant if Max became aggressive. That squawk could break the sound barrier.

It must be ten to one now, she hazarded, though she couldn't see because her eyes were tightly scrunched up against the smarting soap. Still bent double over the basin, with her stockinged legs apart and her three-inch heels dug firmly into the cheap lino, she reached out and flapped a hand in the air, searching for the towel.

It was put into her hand.

Everything froze except her brain. *Max!* She knew it!

Shivers went down her spine. The sinews in her legs became taut. She felt the clenching of the muscles in her buttocks. The stiffening of her naked back.

And then came the stomach-churning thought that Max was probably noticing the tell-tale changes of panic in her body with huge amusement. The women he knew would have given a little wiggle and invited his touch, while she was going pink with embarrassment and ruining any chance she'd had of presenting herself as a city-wise sophisticate.

'Don't get cold, now,' he admonished with a chuckle.

Cold! She was consumed by hell fire in embarrassment!

It seemed safer to stay where she was than to straighten and offer him a full-frontal view. Her hand curled into a claw, snatching the towel away and flinging it over her near nudity.

Max's well-remembered, elegant fingers straightened out the folds with a lingering precision which made her want to scream. He was recreating those days when he hadn't been able to keep his hands off her and had devoted himself to cherishing her. Or so he'd pretended. Max was a master at giving women what they wanted. He found it the quickest route to their beds, so she'd been told.

His distressed parents had explained his tactics. He fitted his behaviour to whichever woman he wanted. For her, he'd been protective, thoughtful, dedicated. He had, *apparently*, found it perfectly possible to be in the same room as Fay and not be dazzled because he'd found, so he'd said, Laura's button nose and higgledy-piggledy mouth absolutely adorable.

Liar.

Laura was struggling for words and sounded almost incoherent when a few managed to crawl out. 'What the *hell*—?'

'I did knock,' came Max's classy drawl, smooth with phoney innocence.

'But didn't wait!' she accused, beside herself with anger at the invasion of her privacy.

'I never do,' he agreed cheerfully.

No. Not for anyone or anything. What Max wanted, he wanted now—or he walked away and found the next most pleasing substitute.

'Well, you can this time. Go back and sit down and wait—or keep walking out of my flat door and don't come back!' she cried, rubbing her face hard in temper with a riskily released corner of the towel.

'You've got five minutes,' he drawled. 'I'm in a hurry.'

'Go and feed the parrot,' she suggested maliciously, knowing Fred would bite off Max's finger if he tried.

'No, thanks.' There was a lazy amusement in his voice. 'It looks diseased.'

Laura pummelled her wet breasts with the towel as if she were kneading bread, furious on her pet's behalf. Somewhere in the background she was aware of the sound of Max's retreating steps.

'By the way,' he called back as an afterthought. 'There's a ladder exploring your left thigh.'

Laura clapped a hand to the back of her leg. He was right. Red-faced and breathing hard, she clutched the towel securely around her and turned in a violent movement to find that he'd vanished.

She loathed him. He made her want to lash out, to slap that arrogant, smoothie face. To knock him off-balance with a step-by-step explanation of what he'd done to her, with all the gory details.

It beggared belief that he was here to make a shameful admission—and yet was strolling around casually, quite unperturbed by the fact that he ought to be ashamed of his actions.

One day, Max Pendennis…one day! she promised vehemently. Then she felt exasperated with herself. In the back of her mind, she'd wanted to appear cool and collected, the epitome of a woman who couldn't care less what he did. Yet already he'd got her stamping mad. Her eyes sparked angrily and she tried to haul down her temper from the stratosphere.

All she had to do was listen to him with a superior smile hovering on her face, make sure that he wasn't going to ruin Fay's marriage by telling Daniel what had happened, and then show him the door.

She decided not to tell him about her pregnancy. She had no intention of playing the sad victim. Her preference was to appear remote, dignified and unassailable…

And yet, she thought, her sense of humour briefly reasserting itself, she'd opened up the proceedings with a classic girlie-magazine pose, presenting her flimsily clad backside, suspenders and stocking-tops to him!

'Three minutes, and counting.'

Laura sent a hot-poker glare at the only bit of him she could see, a pair of long, male legs in soft silver-grey suiting crossed at the ankles, and two glassily polished black shoes.

He was sitting in her favourite easy chair, facing the bed and wardrobe, like someone waiting for the next show to begin.

She stalked into the room just as he was reaching down from the chair to pick up the discarded grey jersey dress. Without a word she took it from him, suddenly conscious of the homely untidiness around her.

There were piles of half-read paperbacks near his feet and a stack of various friends' letters stuffed into the chair beside him. Evidence of her studying lay scattered on every available surface—papers, files, pens, notepads. Max hated mess.

Avoiding contact with his eyes, she stepped over his outstretched legs, toed the daily paper under the small table to join the parrot's tinkly bell and headed for the wardrobe.

All too late, she realised that she'd been clutching the towel around her so tightly that her figure must have been perfectly outlined for him. She eased her neurotic grip, giving him a few more folds to deal with.

Max inhaled audibly behind her as if exasperated.

'If you want me to hurry up,' she said haughtily over her shoulder, 'then face the other way. I'm not dressing while you look on.'

'It would save time if you stayed as you are.' The words slid over her like smooth icing from a spoon. 'It makes no difference to me what you're wearing—'

'Well, it does to me!' she snapped, and regretted losing control. Again. Giving herself a mental kick for her stupidity, she waited haughtily for him to make a move.

The sigh of irritation was repeated, and then there was a scraping sound as the chair was pushed back. When she checked in the mirror, she saw that he was gazing out of the window and standing a disease-free distance from Fred, who was pacing up and down his perch and measuring his chances of a crafty nip.

Satisfied, she opened the wardrobe door, Max's reflected image filling her head.

Tall. Hair still a gleaming raven-black like hers. But the thick waves had been tamed and cut to ruthless perfection, as if his barber had painstakingly worked with a ruler, measuring the requisite distance from that razor-edged white collar.

Max had wider shoulders than she remembered, poured into a sharply tailored suit which had clearly been built on his hard, sinewy body, inch by perfect inch. His spare frame was not heavy with grossly inflexible muscle, but powerfully shaped nevertheless, like that of an athlete in his prime.

He looked breathtakingly handsome. But then he'd always been that—mooned over by her schoolfriends on the rare occasions he'd come home from his prep and then public schools. Son of the wealthy General William Pendennis. Bright future in the City. Every girl's dream—hers included.

Except...he wasn't her Max any more, and hadn't been for a long time. He belonged in a different sphere. A world of privilege and class, peopled by well-bred, elite movers-and-shakers. A world at large which embraced big business, financial deals and where international flights were far more commonplace than number nine buses.

Perhaps aware that she hadn't moved for a few moments, he began drumming his fingers on the high windowsill and tapping his foot. Max hated being cooped up as much as he hated being kept waiting, she reflected, pushing hangers about aimlessly. He was the most restless and active man she'd ever known.

'Will you step on it?' he complained impatiently. 'I've got a flight to catch—and you have one hell of a lot to organise.'

'I have?' That didn't sound as if he was planning a confession about his relationship with Fay—and the consequences. Puzzled, Laura heaved the towel around her top half, grabbed her best suit from the wardrobe and slid the short, straight skirt up over her slender hips. Instantly she felt prim and efficient. 'You'd better talk while I dress, then,' she advised edgily.

His persistent drumming and tapping was driving her mad. She felt a dangerous shakiness creeping into her voice, and tried to calm down. Steeling herself, she flung down the gauntlet.

'Tell me about you and Fay,' she ordered.

'Me and...?'

Jerking her head around, alerted by his astonishment, she found that he was facing her, meeting her startled gaze with a hard, uncomprehending stare. She recoiled, shaken. Partly, if she was honest, by the unexpected head-on impact of his stunning good looks.

'That's why you're here, isn't it?' she demanded, refusing to let him intimidate her. *He* was the one in the wrong! Was he now going to deny the whole affair? 'Losing courage to speak? Don't make me despise you more than I already do, Max,' she muttered.

His dark eyes narrowed but she realised he hadn't heard a word. For the first time he was scrutinising her still puffy eyes fringed with wet black lashes, her tousled hair and unevenly pink and white skin, fresh from its brutal assault at the basin.

She stared back at the pure lines of his sculpted jaw and tried not to feel crushed by his assessment, and horribly unattractive.

'What the devil's been happening to you?'

The softly spoken concern wriggled briefly beneath her defences. Then she remembered. He didn't really care a jot. This was how he got women sewing on his buttons.

'Nothing. A busy morning,' she replied crossly, struck by the ruthless perfection of his grooming and the messiness of hers. Already he'd lowered her self-esteem.

Desperate not to let it sink further, she straightened the slipping towel around her tiny body, turned back to the mirror and grabbed a brush. As she forced it through her tangled mop, she longed for her hair to miraculously turn into a smooth, sophisticated style for once.

She could see Max watching critically, his arms

folded over his lean, taut torso and the plumb-line-straight navy tie accurately bisecting the advertisement-white shirt.

'I can understand,' he said thoughtfully, 'that the guy downstairs mussed your hair up in that clinch…but who made you cry in the first place?'

Her lip quivered and she pulled it into a grimace. He'd laugh if she said a baby! So she said nothing, not even issuing a denial about the clinch. Her brushing became more frantic, but she only ended up with shiny, fly-away hair which flew away in a multitude of directions.

Her face looked small and defenceless, her short upper lip bowing to form an 'oh' of dismay. Two enormous, wet-fringed eyes stared back at her. She looked as if she'd been stabbed in the heart.

Max didn't let up. 'You and the beefy guy had a row…' He paused in the middle of his surmising, a faint frown on his beautifully tanned forehead. 'About me? Because I was coming here and you'd told him we'd been lovers?' he guessed.

'Don't exaggerate your own importance!' she said, shooting a scornful glance at his reflection.

But she quailed at his piercing, bone-melting assessment and longed to be in full war paint for protection. She picked up a tube of all-in-one foundation and powder and began to spread it with shaking, ice-cold fingers.

'You were kissing and—'

'No! That's a lie!'

Disastrously forgetting her intention to stay composed, Laura whirled around indignantly, her eyes glowing fiercely in anger, hair flying about her briefly animated face in jet black tendrils. The wild gipsy look, he'd once said admiringly, before he'd crushed her soft, poppy-coloured mouth beneath his.

For a moment there was a flash of intense light in Max's eyes. She felt it searing a path straight for her

soul. But she was dead inside and it didn't reach anywhere important. He didn't even know he was projecting
sexual desire, she thought peevishly. It was as natural to
him as breathing.

'Too vehement a response, Laura,' he declared quietly. 'I saw you quite clearly. And why shouldn't you
hug and kiss him? Unless...' His mouth became a tight
snarl. 'Unless he's married, of course?'

She couldn't help widening her eyes at his deduction.
'He owns the business,' she said evasively, for something to say.

'And he employs you,' Max persisted, in a savage
undertone, contempt rippling through his harsh features.
'He gives you a flat—'

'It's a bedsit!' she declared. 'Of the non-swinging-cat
variety! And I pay for it. *And* I get up at five to start the
ovens—'

'It's very convenient,' he agreed disparagingly.

She fell silent. He was going to think the worst of her,
but she wasn't going to keep protesting her innocence.
What was the point? In half an hour or so Max would
be out of her life again. She hoped.

His lashes dropped, and she realised he was watching
the way the first curves of her pinkly shining breasts rose
and fell above the failing towel. They went pinker still
and her skin prickled as if he'd switched on an electric
current in her body.

She turned her back on him and rummaged in a
drawer for her shirt, drawing it on and securing the first
two buttons before replying.

'I don't owe you any explanation of my behaviour,'
she said flatly.

'No. You don't. So long as you don't ask for any
explanation of mine.'

They were getting closer to the confession. He felt
ashamed of two-timing her. *Good!*

Triumphantly she finished doing up the last button—only to find it wasn't the last button at all. She had one left over. Annoyed, she started again. Doggedly she worked her way down, her fingers fumbling because he'd moved to one side and was watching every move she made. Her breathing thickened—or the air did; she wasn't sure.

'Are you ready to listen now?' Max asked.

'Perfectly.'

She made sure she spoke in a clipped tone. From now on she'd be detached. He wasn't used to women showing no interest in him and it pleased her that, despite looking and sounding devastatingly handsome and sexy, he'd roused no deep, lingering desires.

A little more confidently, she tucked the shirt in and arranged her small body primly in a threadbare wing chair. Legs neatly crossed at the ankles. Back erect. Distantly involved expression on her face.

'Fire away,' she said, with all the appearance of a woman about to hear something boring. But she felt she might snap at any moment.

Max began wandering about and fingering everything he came across. 'I hope you realise I should be in Paris.'

Absently he stroked the gleaming top of the cluttered mahogany sewing table which had once belonged to her grandmother. He seemed absorbed by the feel of the highly polished wood, his whole face responding to the satiny sensuousness beneath his fingertips. It was a very hedonistic action and had Laura's gaze glued to every lingering caress.

She heaved her mind back to his remark. 'Of course I didn't. Paris, you say?' she asked, intending to sound rudely uninterested, but her remark came out with croaky edges. She cleared her throat as surreptitiously as possible.

Max gave her a look of lazy curiosity and she hardened her eyes in case he got the wrong idea. 'I've had to cancel two meetings.'

He moved lithely on to the mantelpiece, nonchalant and loose-limbed. Casually he began to examine a china herring-gull her mother had sent her. Laura wriggled, uncomfortable with the way he delicately traced the smooth curves of the beautiful bird.

'Must be important news, then,' she encouraged him.

'You can say that again. One of these days, your sister will go too far!'

'I thought she already had,' Laura retaliated, wishing he wouldn't *prowl* so. It made her feel restless. And it set off his long, sinewy legs and lean thighs too well.

He was already on the other side of the room, his hands thrust in his pockets, shoulders hunched as he brooded at her. Such an electric force field surrounded him that, by moving around, he was filling her tiny bedsit with his energy. If he carried on much longer she'd begin to feel suffocated by it.

'Daniel rang me,' Max said sternly.

'I thought you and your brother hadn't spoken since the day he married my sister,' she remarked, lacing her voice with asperity.

Family feuds were so stupid in her view, and Max was small-minded where Fay was concerned. He owed her sister more courtesy than a flat rejection of her existence.

But then, Fay had said he was carrying a torch for her. Max wouldn't have liked being superseded by his less prepossessing brother.

Max grunted. 'I've been funding Daniel for the last few years.'

'Oh. That's very brotherly of you.' She waited while Max did his best to wear out her cheap carpet.

'I did it for the kids.'

She stiffened. Was he going to say more? 'So you
should—'

'But,' he went on, snapping out the word and glaring
at her for interrupting, 'it seems I was funding something
else.' He came to a halt in front of her, his face unnervingly grim.

'Wh-what do you mean?' she asked, prompted by his
air of utter disgust.

Her sister had done some stupid things in her time.
She and Daniel acted like flower-children, wandering
around the country with travellers in battered old vans
and defying authority.

'Daniel and Fay have been arrested,' Max said starkly.

Her heart sank. 'Trespass? Again?' she ventured, remembering she'd had to bail Fay out last time for refusing to leave some farmer's land.

'You don't understand.' Max's mouth tightened as if
he didn't want to continue. His shoulders lifted and
stayed high while she stared at him anxiously, then he
said, punching out the words with barely contained anger, 'They're in jail in Marrakesh.'

Her eyes widened and her mouth fell open in sheer
astonishment as his rage became clear. She knew how
much he hated Daniel's way of life. He was furious with
his brother for blotting the family name. It was all right
to get village girls pregnant and dump them, that was
what the squirearchy did for kicks, but jail was unthink-
able.

'For...what?' she asked breathlessly, her whole attention on his narrowed, glittering eyes.

'Possession of drugs.'

'Oh, God!'

She slumped heavily into the chair, staring into space,
appalled.

'There's no time for histrionics—' he began testily.

'What histrionics? Did you see histrionics?' she

seethed through tightly clenched teeth. 'I was thinking about the children. What's happened to them? And what can we do about getting Fay and Daniel out—?'

'Nothing,' he said brutally.

'*Nothing?* But—'

He silenced her with a scowl and a wipe-out gesture of his expressive hands. 'The kids are the first priority.'

'Of course, but—'

'Listen, will you?' he snapped tetchily.

'You've had time to get used to this!' she protested. 'I'm just trying to get my head around what's happened. OK. So who's looking after Perran and Kerenza now?'

'A traveller friend who's now got tired of playing mothers and fathers.'

Her mind reeled. 'In Marrakesh?'

'No. Port Gaverne.'

Laura's mouth fell open again. 'But that's in Cornwall!' He gave her a slow, mocking hand-clap, making her feel stupid. 'I don't understand…are you telling me…Fay's in Marrakesh and she left her children in *Cornwall*? How could she go away when Kerenza's only a few months old?'

'She's not noted for her devotion to domesticity,' Max said in a grim and disapproving voice.

Laura secretly agreed. She loved Fay, but her sister's behaviour was beyond her. They'd always been chalk and cheese. If *she* had a four-year-old and a baby she'd have to be torn away from them. But then, if something came easy you didn't value it—and Fay had always bemoaned the ease with which she fell pregnant and how the kids hampered her freedom. Laura lowered her eyes to hide the pain. She'd love her freedom to be hampered.

'Well, thanks for telling me,' she said woodenly.

'Someone had to.'

'Presumably the children are at your parents' house right now?'

Max gave her an odd look. 'My mother and father don't live in the manor any more. They've moved to Scotland. The kids are staying in the cottage my father gave Daniel.' He began quartering the floor again, clearly impatient to impart all the details and then go. 'Not that he's ever used it much. It's been rented out most of the time, so goodness knows what kind of state it's in.'

She remembered it. A tiny white stone building set into the side of a cliff. A narrow road ran down from it to the narrow inlet which formed Port Gaverne Bay, the less populated community next to the more bustling Port Isaac, where she'd been brought up, the child of a fisherman.

Fay loathed the cottage. She said it wasn't big enough for a rat—and couldn't the old man have done better than that. The Pendennis family had lived in Pendennis Manor then, further up Port Gaverne Valley. Fay had been hoping for something similar.

'I'm sure it's fine,' Laura said, not sure at all.

She studied a slender leg, thoughtfully. This was a different kind of news from the sort she'd been expecting. Her face grew dreamy. Images came to her: sunny blue skies, glittering waves, dark cliffs. The smell of the sea was so real that she could almost taste the salt on her lips. For a moment she felt the spring of sea pinks beneath her feet, and then there was nothing other than the thin, worn lino.

She smiled faintly, wistfully. 'Perran is probably having a great time on the beach every day—'

'He'll be there on his own by tomorrow morning,' Max informed her sourly. 'The friend is off to some music festival.' He seemed as edgy as she was about the situation.

'Well, that's out! She can't leave the children!' Laura protested, bristling with indignation.

He shrugged. 'The woman wasn't paid to babysit. Why should she stay?'

'Because they're in need!' she spluttered, amazed at people's lack of responsibility.

'She's adamant about going. I don't blame her. Fay promised they'd only be gone two days on a trip to London, and it's now two weeks. She deliberately lied. Your sister isn't too familiar with the truth, is she?'

Laura wished she could defend Fay. Her sister was wonderful fun to be with, but not very grounded in the real world. 'I'm sure there's a good reason—'

'There is. Fay's not cut out to be a mother and the children hinder her activities,' Max said drily.

She winced. 'What's to be done?' she asked, concentrating on the practical.

Max paused and lifted a black eyebrow. He seemed to be fixated on her softly parted mouth. She closed it and swallowed, bringing his gaze to her throat. Warmth stole over her skin and she knew she was flushing like a stupid schoolgirl. Angry with herself, she set her teeth and fixed her gaze somewhere in the mid-distance.

'Isn't that obvious?' he observed smoothly. 'If someone doesn't get down there to take over, the kids'll be dumped on the beach and abandoned.'

Laura wasn't slow. She could see where this was leading. It was written all over his face. So she pre-empted him. 'And you're going down to look after them,' she said, giving him what she imagined to be an admiring look. 'Very good of you—'

'It's not good at all. *You're* going.'

She looked at him steadily. No way. It was a suggestion so far into the stratosphere that she didn't even fear it would come true.

She'd vowed never to return. Nor would she get involved with her sister's children. She'd never even seen them. Kerenza was a baby. The other...

Perran was Max's child.

CHAPTER TWO

SHE'D feared that Max had found out and had come to claim his rights as a father. Instead, he was asking her to look after his own son and a little baby! Perhaps he didn't know about Perran after all!

'I can't. I have my job,' she explained, proud to be as cool as a cucumber.

'OK.'

To her surprise, he made no attempt to argue but headed straight for the door. She gaped at him. Was that it?

'What are you going to do about the children?' she cried in astonishment.

'Me?' Max half turned, presenting his clean-cut profile. 'I saw that as your responsibility. If you're not interested, well...there it is. I'll let you know the phone number of the Home they're in—'

'Home? What do you mean "Home"?' she yelled, jumping up.

'It's a place where orphans or children at risk go—'

'I *know* what a Home is!' she hurled. 'You know what I meant—don't be so obtuse! You couldn't possibly contemplate the idea of putting your own nephew and niece into care.'

'What other options are there?' With infuriating rationality he ticked off the reasons for his conclusion on his long, lean fingers. 'You won't go, I can't go, so they've got to be cared for by the State, since you're not keen to let them live on the street and raid dustbins.' Quite unconcerned, he put his hand out to open the door.

Laura was there before he made contact, sliding herself between him and the thin chipboard. He had no heart. Since he was his own boss, he could easily take time off to care for his son and niece. But he wouldn't bother to put himself out, would he? Her face registered its disgust, and when a small smile played about his lips she gave him her fiercest scowl.

'For once in your life,' she said, the pitch and intensity of her voice showing the full force of her anger, 'do something for someone else! For two little children—'

'Ditto back.'

How could he be so unemotional about this? Almost amused! Laura knew she had to persuade him to take on his responsibilities as an uncle. And father.

'I repeat. I have my job—'

'I'm sure Huggy Bear will give you leave under the circumstances,' he said, sublimely relaxed and watching her as though she was unwittingly entertaining him.

Laura glared. 'I've got two twenty-first birthdays, an eightieth and a silver wedding cake to make this week! Plus a business conference with one hundred men demanding treacle sponges and bread puddings!'

'Sounds delicious—'

'Stop patronising me!' she flared. 'I'm not part of some huge operation where someone can go off and not be missed! Luke and I need each other—'

'Yes. I saw.'

Impatient with his curt condemnation, she brushed his sarcasm aside. 'You'll have to cope with the situation. I can't let Luke down.'

'He'd have to manage if you were ill,' Max pointed out, angling his dark head in a 'Mr Reasonable' attitude. 'What would happen then?'

'He'd work overtime or call his sister in to help,' she admitted. 'But I couldn't possibly ask him.'

'Then I will. I doubt he'd refuse. He'd look too churlish, wouldn't he?'

She wondered if Max ever took no for an answer. 'OK! I need the money!' she claimed, abandoning her pride and any pretence that she'd made good. He'd seen the flat, hadn't he? There was no way he'd believe she was madly successful.

'I'll pay you.' Max beamed as though that solved everything.

'I wouldn't take money from you if I was homeless and living in a cardboard box in a multi-storey car park in sub-zero temperatures!' she yelled.

Instead of being suitably offended, he appeared to be fighting down a grin. His eyes positively twinkled at her. 'Stalemate, I think. Unless you have any bright ideas?'

'Yes. You could go and play uncle!' she insisted, feeling hot and bothered.

He shrugged off that idea as ludicrous. 'I'd probably poison them. I don't know anything about kids.'

'Neither do I!' she cried, her voice quavering with emotion.

'No?'

He folded his arms. They brushed against her breasts—and she had nowhere to go except through the chipboard door. She made herself as thin as possible, conscious of the heat building up between them. Her eyes pleaded with his. He didn't budge an inch.

'No. What would I know?' she muttered, trying not to breathe heavily.

The dark eyes kindled with warmth. 'Some women are naturally maternal. You were always looking after the village kids. I called you the Pied Piper, remember?'

Incapable of speech, Laura kept on staring at him as misery gathered like a huge knotted blanket in her throat. Max's voice gentled and his mouth became unfairly soft and tender.

'They hung around you as if you were their idol—'

'No!' she jerked out in surprise, shaking her dark head emphatically.

'Of course you were. Didn't you tell them stories? Invent adventure games? Teach them about the plants and birds and generally mother them—?'

'They were older! Not infants in nappies,' she broke in, harshness masking her distress. 'Seven...nine, ten... I wouldn't know the first thing a-about...'

She felt treacherous tears welling up and got rid of them through sheer will-power, squashing the fact that she'd boned up on babies once by reading everything she could lay her hands on. She'd wiped all that from her mind. She couldn't look after little Kerenza. She just *couldn't*. It would break her heart.

'It'd come to you, what to do. You're a woman,' Max said, transparently pleased with his logic.

'Oh, for heaven's sake!' she spat, livid with fury.

He touched her rigid shoulder lightly and she jerked his hand off with unaccustomed violence, the calming, protective sensation quite unnerving her.

'I'm not being chauvinistic,' he murmured. 'Your sister aside, women have instincts. They're genetically programmed to be caring and tender, and they notice things that we men would miss—'

'Then you'll just have to try harder, dig down deep and search for some stray shred of love and tenderness and apply it to this situation, won't you?' she flung.

'Meaning?' he asked quietly, his eyes boring into hers.

It delighted her that he'd been offended at last. 'I think I'm being as clear as crystal. Work at it. Find your heart, crank it up and use it. It'd do you good.'

'Hmm.' For a brief moment, she thought Max was contemplating the idea. Then he shook his head. 'It wouldn't work. I've got no yardstick. I wouldn't know about bedtimes or what to feed them.' He adopted an earnest, searching look. 'When can babies eat chips and stuff?'

'You're not that ignorant!' she scathed. 'Ask the fed-up friend when you get there. Do your charming act and she'll willingly clue you up. In fact she'll probably stay to help.'

He gave a short laugh. 'Thanks for your faith in my powers of persuasion.'

'You don't need any abilities. You're just good-looking,' she snapped. 'You don't have to do anything, just stand about in masculine poses and look gorgeous.' Appalled at her bitchiness, shamed by his stony silence, she blamed her venom on her shredded nerves.

'Isn't that look-ist or something?' he asked tautly.

'Not when it's true. You've always relied on your appearance to get what you want.'

He studied her with interest, a dangerous glint in his dark, almost luminous eyes. 'Shall we explore that statement further?' he suggested, with menace lurking in every word.

'No. I want to get the children settled!' she replied, two glowing splashes of colour on her cheeks. The last thing she wanted was a rerun of her helpless crush on him. 'Max, give it a try,' she pleaded. 'You know you could persuade the friend to stay.'

'Perhaps,' he conceded. 'Though I doubt it would be a good move. If she's prepared to abandon the kids, then she's the usual sort of person Fay and Daniel gather around them.'

'You can't generalise…'

'I'm drawing a reasonable conclusion, given the facts,' he drawled. 'Fay attracts people like her. Fickle. *Fey*. It wouldn't surprise me if this friend doesn't have the first idea about looking after children. Laura, I know from what Daniel told me that you've never seen the kids—'

'Have *you*?' she shot back, so sensitive about that fact that she took his remark for a reproach.

'No. I imagine we've missed out for the same reasons. Fay and Daniel have spent the whole of their married life travelling around the back lanes of Britain and picking up their welfare cheques. It's been almost impossible to keep in touch. Laura, think about this again. Perran would be easily catered for. Treat him as if he's older, like a seven-year-old without any sense. As for Kerenza, well, babies sleep and eat a lot...don't they?' he asked uncertainly. 'If your sister can cope, anyone can. I'm sure it's no big deal, looking after them.'

'I have a better idea. Your best bet is to employ a nanny. Go down and make friends with the children then introduce the nanny—make sure she's kind,' she said anxiously, 'and—'

'A nanny! That's a brilliant idea!' he said, much to her surprise. 'Only...there's a flaw in it. I wouldn't have the first idea about the qualities a nanny should have,' Max admitted. He studied her anxious, uptight figure and suddenly seemed to be hit by inspiration. 'Wait a minute!' he cried, his face creasing into smiles.

Laura took the full force of his charisma and felt a sucking sensation in the pit of her stomach. 'Why should I?' she asked ungraciously.

'I have a compromise solution.' He extended the smile to one of his dazzling grins.

She frowned, knowing perfectly well that he believed he could get anything from anyone if he just put on that open-faced, beguiling expression.

'What?'

'We both go down to Cornwall—'

'Both? You and me?' she squeaked, aghast.

'I wasn't thinking of asking Luke!' he replied, his eyes sparkling with humour.

'The answer's no.'

'Laura, we can reassure the children and hand out sweets or whatever you do—'

'No.'

'And stay till we've found a nanny with your help—'

'No!' Would he never accept that as her answer?

'That couldn't possibly take more than a few days,' he went on, unwittingly responding to her silent question. 'I'll then fly to Marrakesh and pull a few strings so Daniel and Fay are released.' And, with what was plainly a carefully judged, coaxing smile, he added softly, 'It's either that or the children must go into care. I leave it to you to decide.'

'Oh, thanks.'

He didn't know what he was asking. He wanted her to look after his son. She might as well stick knives into herself and be done with it.

She stared gloomily at her feet. From his casualness about Perran's welfare, it was obvious that Max *didn't* know he was the boy's father. Fay had kept her secret and that was a small consolation.

But...it would be a terrible strain to do what he suggested. She'd be cooped up in a tiny cottage with Max, his child, and a little baby. More worrying, she'd want to cuddle the children and love them—but if she did she'd get terribly hurt.

She'd be forced to watch Max taking his turn—because she'd insist—in rocking the children to sleep or reading them bedtime stories. Simulated parenthood. The reality she could never have. The situation would be too poignant and it would create too many new scars.

No. Impossible.

A few days of longing, heartache, loving. Then emptiness again. The ultimate in masochism.

'What's it to be? Your needs or theirs?' drawled Max cruelly.

Her spiky black lashes flicked up and there was a mute appeal in her brimming Wedgwood-blue eyes.

'I—I...can't! I—' Her voice cracked up and she jammed shut her trembling mouth.

Max's superficially genial expression changed in an instant. Charm was replaced by tensile steel. 'It's Luke, isn't it?' he demanded roughly. 'God! You're faced with a choice between your sister's kids and your boyfriend and you choose him? He means that much to you?'

'Stop browbeating me! I have to think this through,' she said shakily, abandoning her door-barring pose and walking with unnatural care to sit tensely on the arm of a chair.

'How long do you need to decide?' he demanded.

'I don't *know*!'

'It's at least a five-hour drive there,' he pointed out in grim tones. 'I'd like us to leave in a few minutes. The friend ought to introduce us to Perran before his bedtime. The kiddie would be bewildered and frightened if he woke to find two strangers in the house claiming to be his aunt and uncle.'

So he did have some human concern after all. And he was right. She had to make a snap decision. Her hand wove its way through her hair, mussing it up thoroughly. Her heart was leaping erratically at the prospect that she'd be playing mummies and daddies with Max.

Unable to cope, she slid sideways into the chair and landed with a thump. Untangling her legs and twitching her short skirt back in place, she said with a weird huskiness, 'You're asking too much.'

'No.' Max folded his arms. 'Your sister is. She always does.'

'You really dislike her, don't you?' she accused.

'Utterly.'

She glared at his uncompromising agreement. It had been Daniel who'd led Fay astray, Daniel who'd got them into the travelling scene and introduced Fay to drugs. Fay had told her everything.

'What about your brother?' she said, rounding on Max, determined not to let an injustice pass. 'He could have stopped this jaunt if he'd wanted. He's equally guilty of deserting his children for his own selfish needs—'

'You're evading the issue,' Max reminded her. He pulled out an ultra-slim mobile phone from his inside breast pocket. 'I'm not wasting any more valuable time. I can ring Directory Enquiries and get the children's officer to go along and pick the kids up. They'll be off our hands. An easy solution. What do you think?'

'You brute!'

'Practical, though.' He began to punch numbers. 'Hello? Directory Enquiries…?'

She shuddered, staring into space. Perran was only four. A total stranger would haul him and his baby sister off to live in some regimented institution. However caring it might be, she doubted that Fay had ever imparted any discipline to her children and it would be a total culture shock.

He rang off, a piece of paper in his hand with a phone number hastily scrawled on it. 'Do I call them or not?'

A heaviness claimed her limbs as she slumped further in the seat. She had no option. Whatever her feelings, the needs of the children came first. She'd do her best for their sakes.

Pale and tense, her eyes almost silver as she tried to face the stark choice she was having to make, she met Max's inscrutable gaze and steeled herself to the decision.

'I'll have to take my parrot.'

Max visibly relaxed. 'You can take the entire contents of this flat, if you like, but get moving!'

She felt the whole of her body shaking. She was so weak that she knew it would be an effort to get up.

'Just Fred,' she said in a small, unhappy voice.

'You'll be back before you know it,' Max said gruffly. 'Do you want to ring your mother and let her know?'

'She's in New Zealand,' Laura said, her face soft with affection. And, knowing Max would be astonished that her mother had left her beloved Cornwall, added, 'She met a tourist from Auckland a couple of years ago and fell in love. They're very happy.'

'I'm very pleased—and not at all surprised. She's a lovely lady. Very caring, well-liked.' He paused. 'So there's only Luke here for you. I can imagine,' he conceded, 'how you feel, having to leave someone you care for.' There was a moment's silence as though he was thinking of something in his own past. 'Still, look on the bright side—Luke will realise how much he misses you. That's always good for a relationship between lovers, isn't it?'

She stared at him dumbly. Leaving aside the fact that she didn't *have* that kind of a relationship with Luke, no, it wasn't a good thing. When men went away they found new partners. You couldn't trust them. Out of sight, out of mind. She was so miserable that she didn't bother to disillusion him about Luke. She didn't have the energy.

'I'd better tell him,' she said wearily.

He put up a hand to stop her. 'No. I'll explain. You pack. I want to get on the road immediately—we've wasted too much time haggling as it is.'

'You really believed I'd leap at the chance to babysit, didn't you?' Resentful of his assumption and bossiness, Laura heaved herself out of the chair.

'Of course I did. You always adored kids. I'm surprised you haven't had any,' he said, striding to the door and thus not noticing her expression of anguish. 'Throw some things into a case and I'll be up to carry your stuff down while you're saying your goodbyes to Huggy Bear.'

Laura doubled over when he'd gone, burying her face in her hands. She felt ice-cold and sick. This was going to be worse than she'd thought.

For a few moments she breathed deeply. It didn't do much for her wobbly legs, but the nausea eased. Experimentally she staggered to her feet and, barely able to walk a straight line, she dragged out her suitcase from under the bed. And stared at it helplessly, the seconds and minutes ticking away in the silence.

The last time she'd used the case had been for her escape from Port Isaac, pregnant, afraid, bound for her aunt's house in distant London—a city she'd never visited in her whole, unworldly life. So scared, so miserable and ashamed...

Her mother had stayed to keep an eye on Fay. Not very successfully...

So much had happened since then. She knelt on the floor, remembering how desperately lonely she'd felt. The week before she'd fled, Max had gone to Paris on business and his parents had turned up, their kind faces full of sympathy for her as they'd explained about the beautiful, sophisticated fiancée waiting for him and how upset they were that Max had sown his wild oats with a decent village girl.

Almost immediately afterwards she'd known she was pregnant. Swearing her mother and Fay to secrecy, she'd gone to London. The noise, the traffic, the greyness had punched into her like a fist. She'd cried herself to sleep every night with homesickness.

'Need help?'

'Oh, Luke, I—!' Longing to confide her fears, she turned around in an almost desperate relief—and then clammed up.

Max was standing next to her boss, a tight frown of irritation on his handsome face. He looked taut, poised like a wound-up spring ready to snap, an air of grim determination about him as if he was coming to a major decision about something then and there.

'Luke says it's OK for you to go.'

He met her eyes in an unspoken challenge. She shrank back, suddenly afraid. When her glance slanted to Luke, she was aware that Max's chest inflated with an inexplicable anger. It couldn't be jealousy—what did he care? Something else, then. Laura swallowed nervously, drawn back to Max's face as if by a magnet.

The contrast between the two men was striking. Luke, for all his size, seemed to pale into insignificance, dwarfed by Max's compelling darkness.

Her eyes remained fixed on Max's beautifully sculpted features even when Luke came over and knelt beside her, taking her hands in his.

'Do you think you can cope?' he asked quietly.

'I'll be fine—'

'I'm not asking her to run an orphanage single-handed!' scathed Max.

Laura raised her eyes comically to heaven to show Luke that she was equal to anything Max threw at her. 'Known for his charm,' she said drily, and Luke grinned in transparent relief. She leapt to her feet, determined not to show her true emotions. 'Right. Get Fred into his travelling cage,' she ordered Max, 'while I pack and tell Luke about the cakes I was supposed to be baking.'

'I've got the list.' Luke lumbered to his feet too, and pulled the paper from his pocket. 'I'll manage fine.'

There was a furious screech from Fred and an even angrier one from Max. Serves him right, Laura thought, and turned around, all innocent enquiry.

'Did he bite?' she asked, inanely, since Max was sucking his knuckle and hurling a look to kill at Fred.

'You know damn well he did,' Max said, flashing her a look of pure menace from beneath his black brows.

Luke exchanged glances with Laura and chuckled, then ambled over and coochie-cooed Fred, who did his little dance and meekly stepped onto Luke's hand.

'In you go,' he said. 'I'll get his food tin, shall I, Laura?'

'Please,' she answered vaguely, grabbing handfuls of underwear and flinging them in the direction of her case before moving on to the wardrobe. Old jumpers, jeans…they found their way—well, almost their way—to the suitcase.

When she'd finished and began collecting up her wash bag and make-up, she found that Max was grimly folding her clothes and organising everything sensibly, her shoes being neatly stuffed with briefs and bras…

'Max,' she pleaded faintly, disturbed by seeing him touching her most intimate things. 'Leave that!'

'I'm trying to get some urgency into the proceedings!' He shot her a baleful glance. 'Time is ticking away. I think we must leave.'

Feeling as if a lighted fuse was burning inside her, she dragged her jacket on, grabbed her study folder and pushed books into a plastic carrier bag.

'I'm ready.'

They all trooped downstairs with their respective loads, and the two men, bristling like rival dogs, packed the dark-chocolate Range Rover which Max had arrogantly left parked on the pavement. Fred screamed in protest at his disturbed routine until Laura cooed to him and threw the night cover over his cage.

'Say your goodbyes,' Max ordered curtly, his head stuck under the bonnet, checking the oil level.

Luke drew her into the shop out of sight behind the pasty display. Lord! she thought shakily. She'd be eating Cornish-baked ones in a few hours!

'You going to be OK? He said a couple of days—'

'No trouble. I've got his measure,' she pretended. 'And I'm sorry to muck you about. I'll be back as soon as I can.'

'I know that,' reassured Luke. 'I'll be thinking of you. The kiddies need you more than I do. And if you want a friendly ear...' he fumbled in his waistcoat pocket and brought out a card. 'This is my home number. My wife'll be only too glad to chat. She's one in a million, Laura. You can trust her to understand.'

'Thanks. You've been terrific.'

She reached up and gave him a hesitant kiss on the cheek, and hurried out, wondering if she'd ever regain complete control of her legs again.

Max, ever the superficial gentleman whatever his mood, was holding open the car door for her. It was on the driver's side. Tucking Luke's card into her jacket pocket, she looked at him questioningly.

'I have to make a few calls while we're going along,' he explained.

He took her elbow, and she wondered what had made his voice so husky and laced his eyes with...*pain*? That couldn't be right—unless he felt nervous about looking after two children. She hoped he was in for a steep learning curve.

'You drive,' he prompted.

Laura dragged her mind back to his request. 'I can't!'

He was staggered. 'You...can't...*drive*?'

'It's not that unusual, surely? I came here straight from home when I was eighteen, remember?' she replied huffily. He was acting as though driving was essential for anyone who wanted to be regarded as belonging to the human race! 'You don't need a car in London. It's almost *stupid* to have a car in London. There was never the need.'

'Hell.'

He stalked around to the passenger side and waited while she struggled up the high steps, flashing, she was sure, a long length of leg.

Not that it would look at all enticing, she remembered with a silent groan. It would have been taken up almost entirely by a ragged ladder, and she wasn't sure whether she was pleased or dismayed.

They were through Kensington and Chiswick and on the M4 before she'd even steadied her pulses. Max had always been a masterful driver. With every mile they clocked up, his mood lifted a little further and he stopped scowling.

Laura found herself watching how he handled the vehicle, admiring his confidence and quick reactions. He didn't get angry when other drivers vacillated or invented their own versions of the Highway Code, but dealt decisively with each situation as it came up. He'd be good in a crisis, she thought absently. She stored away that information without knowing why.

'OK,' he said, easing himself comfortably in his seat as he cruised past everything in sight. She didn't like the sound of that OK. There was an air of resolution about it. She gripped the edge of her seat and was surprised when all he said was 'Lunch.'

'Are we stopping?' she asked, confused.

'It's in the glove box. I asked Luke to put something in a bag for us.'

Laura cautiously flicked the catch and extracted a 'Saucy Sandwich' carton. Two Cornish pasties, smoked salmon on brown bread sandwiches—probably with lemon—chocolate éclairs and an assortment of chocolate bon bons.

'My favourites! Good old Luke,' she exclaimed fondly.

'To hell with Luke. Feed me,' Max ordered, concentrating on the road.

She sighed audibly, like a martyr forced to do yet another penance, and thrust the pasty in the general direction of his face.

'Break off bits,' he instructed.

Driving seemed to take up all his attention. She'd never seen anyone so intent on the traffic before. Certain that this was part of some game he'd devised, she deliberately passed him a chunk of the crimped end which was just pastry and no filling.

Keeping his eyes on the road, he lifted his hand from the steering wheel and closed it over hers, like Ronald Coleman accepting a cigarette from Bette Davis in an old black and white movie.

She knew now why the two film stars had ignited with the cigarette. It was a very sexy manoeuvre. Max was lifting her hand slowly to his mouth, and she was watching the whole thing in a kind of blurred, suspended excitement.

With breathtaking deliberation, Max's lips closed around the pastry, touching her fingers at the same time with an electrifying warmth. Immediately, she snatched her hand away and bit an inelegant chunk out of her own pasty. Her heart thudded loud enough for him to hear, she felt sure.

'It's very good,' admired Max, licking crumbs from his lips with the tip of his tongue.

'Course it is.'

Laura found herself fascinated by the beautifully-chiselled mouth, gleaming where his tongue had flickered, searching for stray bits of pastry. She jumped guiltily when he glanced at her and said, 'Did you make this?'

With her mouth full, she nodded. 'Mmm.' There seemed to be a wicked twinkle in his eyes and it worried her.

'More.' He almost purred. 'Keep the driver happy.'

Refusing to play his silly game, she broke off a huge piece and pushed it into his mouth. He let her. This time she felt the pressure of his warm lips against her palm. His eyes closed in a brief display of bliss, dark lashes thickly fanning out on his cheeks, his expression suggesting he'd tasted nectar.

'Don't go overboard,' she said tartly. 'It's only a Cornish pasty.'

'I haven't had anything like this for a long time.' A slow, erotic smile curved his mouth. 'Some sensations can't be replicated. This is the genuine thing. Thanks for reminding me what I've missed, Laura.'

Her expression became scornful. He didn't have to go over the top! 'You flatter my cooking ability too much.'

'No, I don't.'

Despite the deep huskiness of his voice, she knew he was praising her for his own ends, not because he found her pastry out of this world.

Max needed to be admired. His parents had explained that to her. He couldn't bear to be disliked or ignored and so he made a supreme effort to win people over. Then he got them running around for him. Then he dumped them because he despised them for falling for his questionable methods. Rat.

She'd felt sorry for the nervous Mrs Pendennis and even sorrier for her gruff husband, who seemed deeply uncomfortable about accusing his elder son of grossly immoral behaviour.

Max didn't know his own parents had condemned him. It must have taken guts for them to do that, and she'd been grateful. She'd rather be alone than with a man she couldn't trust.

'And some more!' He leaned a little to the side, eyes still on the road, his lips slightly parted in readiness for another morsel.

Determined not to fit neatly into whatever slot he'd

allocated for her on this trip, she decided on a put-down as she popped a piece of pasty into his mouth.

'Last time I did this,' she informed him maliciously, 'it was with a doughnut and an elephant.'

He munched for a while, not at all perturbed. Then, with a suspicion of laughter lurking in his off-hand reply, he said, 'Good practice for aiming straight.'

Resisting the urge to plaster pasty over his face—and knowing that would provoke a dangerous revenge on his part—she continued to feed him. When he'd demolished it all with evident satisfaction, and some appreciative murmuring deep in his throat which she found worryingly sexy, he stretched out with one arm and caught her hand again.

'There's nothing left!' she said hastily, and then, 'Oh!'

A high-voltage current had passed through her entire body. He was enthusiastically licking off the flaky pastry which had stuck to her palm and fingers. She gazed at his absorbed face, her heart skittering about unevenly as the air left her lungs at an alarming rate.

'Delicious,' he murmured, and Laura came out of her trance.

'Don't *do* that!' she grumbled, dragging out a hanky and scrubbing her hand vigorously. But her skin wouldn't stop tingling.

'Too good to miss,' he said with toe-curling huskiness.

Laura wasn't sure if he meant the pastry flakes or the chance to unnerve her. Experience told her to favour the second option.

'Have a sandwich!' Ungraciously, she aimed it for his nose, but he avoided it with a quick movement of his head.

'I'll pass, thanks. Never fancied inhaling smoked salmon. Pop a chocolate in my mouth instead, will you?

And be accurate. We don't want to have an accident, do we?'

Laura's eyes hardened. Ronald Coleman had never gone that far. Breathing heavily in anger, she tipped Max's share onto the ledge of the dashboard.

'Help yourself,' she said grumpily. Then in a moment of mischief announced, 'Luke made these.'

'Known him long?' he asked, selecting a chocolate.

'Long enough.'

His strong teeth cracked the toffee centre neatly in half. 'Nice guy,' he said without conviction.

'He is. Terribly nice.' Hah! she thought. Probe as much as you like. You won't get anything out of me. She remembered the fiancée in Surrey. 'What about your personal life? Are you married with...' she tried to sound normal '...two point four children?'

'My personal life is like yours. Personal.'

He took out a searingly white handkerchief with razor creases and wiped his mouth. Laura found herself wondering who did his ironing. Someone devoted to him or with nothing better to do, she decided. She made it a rule never to iron hankies—life was too short.

'We'll stop for a coffee later,' he went on. 'Eat the rest. I've had enough.'

'So've I.'

Her appetite had vanished at the possibility that Max might have a family. She pictured him gazing at his first-born, torturing herself with 'if onlys'—not that she wanted to be his wife. She pitied the poor woman.

Then Laura recalled that he'd claimed a total ignorance about children. Still, she remembered, hedging her bets, you could never tell with Max if he was spinning a line or not.

'Here.' He held out his mobile phone. 'Press "A", then "one", and when someone answers hold it up to my ear.'

'No, thanks. I'd rather wait till we stop,' she suggested, loath to play Bette Davis again.

'Laura, we're using this time to ring my office, cancel my Paris meeting and get my secretary to ring round the nanny agencies,' he said with painstaking care, as if she had an IQ of twenty-four. 'You do want to start interviewing tomorrow, don't you?'

'I do!' she cried fervently, and punched the numbers. The answering voice was warm, friendly and cultured. 'Sue Linley, PA to Max Pendennis; can I help you?'

Laura pushed the phone against Max's ear and listened unashamedly, not even pretending to be otherwise occupied with the scenery as they sped along and the distant battlements and keeps of Windsor Castle disappeared from view.

It sounded a genuinely affectionate relationship. Max bantered with Sue, who gave as good as she got; consequently he spent a lot of time laughing.

Because she was acting as phone-holder, Laura had no choice but to be involved in this merriment. She almost giggled when Sue's disembodied voice crackled out over the ether, suggesting that Max's clothes, intended for a week or so in Paris, would scare the seagulls eggless.

'I've got jeans and jumpers too,' Max said, pretending to be offended.

'Yeah. Ralph Lauren suede and pure cashmere,' replied Sue. 'Great for kneeling on blobs of jam and catching airborne yoghurt.'

Laura threw Max a sidelong glance. He looked a little pale at the prospect ahead. 'Just push a pramful of potential nannies my way *fast*, will you?' he asked, obviously alarmed. 'Get them on the train to Bodmin and I'll collect them. Let me know when. Cheers.'

Laura removed the phone and switched it off. It comforted her that the children would be well cared for soon.

Maybe even by tomorrow afternoon they would have a qualified nanny, and she could return to London, hardly the worse for wear.

She stretched her body, lifting her arms over her head, and then relaxed. 'It's all working out well,' she said, pleased.

'Going to plan.'

Laura shot him a suspicious look. There had been something oddly smug about his comment. 'Both of us will be relieved to get back to normality,' she said nervously, pushing him for confirmation.

'There's nothing I'd like better,' he murmured.

Why would he be almost purring with contentment? He wasn't looking forward to the next forty-eight hours any more than she was. Yet there was now an air of excitement surrounding him, as if he couldn't wait for what lay ahead.

She racked her brains for an explanation but couldn't come up with anything. Laura felt suddenly weary. Not only was she bound for an area choc-a-bloc with hurtful memories and two children who'd do their best to unlock her padlocked heart, but she'd have to deal with whatever Max had in store for her.

Glumly she curled up and shut her eyes. She felt worn out by the stresses of the day and was suddenly afraid of those waiting for her. Max wouldn't be easy to handle. The hairs on the back of her neck rose as he began to hum quietly to himself.

Max had plans. And she figured in them.

A chill went through her which she firmly repressed. If he thought she'd warm his bed for the next two nights, he had another think coming. His learning curve was going to be so steep he'd fall off the end.

Blanking her mind to Max's low, melodious crooning of 'When I Fall in Love', she slowly drifted off into an uneasy sleep.

CHAPTER THREE

THE next thing Laura was conscious of was the sudden cessation of movement. She didn't open her eyes. She wanted to feign sleep till they arrived. Perhaps they had.

'Laura…'

'Are we there?' she asked drowsily, lulled into a delicious lethargy by Max's slow drawing out of her name.

'No. Exeter. I'm bushed. I'm going for a coffee. Coming?'

He was leaning over her, staring into her dreamy eyes. She looked into the big pools of liquid brown and felt a shocking emptiness in her stomach.

'I could eat an elephant,' she pronounced quickly, uncomfortable with the way he was invading her space.

'You have an elephant fixation.'

A faint smile touched the corner of his mouth and then was gone. He moved away, his clothes rustling a little as he did so. It was then that she realised she hadn't heard that sound when she'd woken up.

That meant he'd been leaning over her while she'd slept.

Laura blinked, and her fine brows drew together in puzzlement. Why would he do that? Had she been snoring? Did she have bits of pasty on her nose? Hurriedly she flipped down the vanity mirror and checked.

'You look passable. Good enough for a service station anyway,' Max said cuttingly, getting out of the car and walking around it.

She fiddled with her hair for a while to annoy him then attempted a lithe exit herself. Unfortunately her legs were stiff and unresponsive, and she ended up falling into his arms with a surprised 'Oof!'

They both remained glued together for a heady moment, as if their bodies were welcoming each other home. Then Laura coldly pushed herself away and went to see if Fred was all right.

'He's sleeping,' she said in relief, emerging from the boot and staggering a little as a gust of wind whipped across the car park.

Max steadied her by tucking his hand beneath her elbow, and flicked on the alarm system. 'Lucky him,' he muttered.

Laura felt guilty. His stride had lost its spring and he was evidently tired. But as they entered the self-service restaurant he made the same impact he always did. People quite simply stared.

Oblivious to—or ignorant of—the fact that not every man naturally drew eyes like magnets, he wearily queued for his coffee without even complaining.

Further back, collecting a plate of chips, a ham roll and a strawberry tart, Laura was able to see the effect he had on everyone as he lounged against a counter, waiting for her to catch up.

She had to admit that he did look outstandingly compelling. There was something about his flawlessly smooth skin which urged fingers to reach up for a sinful stroke. The cheekbones in his face were quite prominent, his eyes dark and brooding beneath thick ebony lashes, his mouth relaxed with tiredness into a slightly sulky curve. It made her fantasise about kissing it into laughter for a brief, unguarded moment.

Several other women were definitely weighing up their chances. He was being scanned in detail, from his smooth, jet-black head to the even glossier Italian shoes, with half of Europe's designers making up the classy, throw-away elegance in between. A dish. Exotic...

He scowled at Laura and she saw he was tapping his foot. Annoyed to be caught gaping, she adopted a look of indifference and swept past the gawping crowd just as a girl in an overall dashed past her and flung herself into the neighbouring till.

'Like to come over, sir?' the cashier called breathily.

Sir did. Laura joined him and pushed her tray next to his, watching in resignation while the girl carried on an animated conversation with him, ignoring her completely. During which, to do him credit, he managed to make a few courteous contributions.

'I think I might need a sleep before we drive on,' he informed Laura, when they'd found a vacant table. 'I only had a couple of hours' shut-eye on the flight over in the early hours of this morning. I was banking on us sharing the driving.'

He leaned back and rested an arm along the top of the bench seat, throwing her a lopsided smile warm enough to melt her heart.

Something happened there, to be sure. This vulnerable man with strain-crinkled eyes and loose, relaxed limbs was more appealing to her than her impression of an arrogant, domineering Max who'd callously dumped her.

'I'll get a paper to read while you have a rest, then,' she said. Her voice sounded soft and husky. She wondered if she should toughen it up.

Long ago, she'd had a blueprint in her brain of her ideal partner. She'd thought Max had fitted it perfectly. They'd got on so well. Same zany sense of humour, same love for the wild Cornish coast, same enjoyment of the simple pleasures in life.

For reasons of his own, he appeared to be trying hard to match up to the man he'd once pretended to be—but there was a difference this time. She knew he was faking.

Max sipped his coffee, watching her over the rim of

his cup. His eyes were disarmingly friendly. 'Mind if I steal a chip?'

'You'll get spots.'

'Doesn't stop you.'

'I'm beyond all hope,' she said expansively.

He smiled. 'I don't think so.'

Despite the banality of the conversation, her heart was pumping harder than usual. The envious glances in her direction were making the situation more intimate than it should have been. Everyone was assuming that they belonged to one another. It made her feel odd.

Casually glancing around the restaurant and pretending not to notice the attention Max was getting, she waded into the chips herself. Travelling always made her feel inordinately hungry.

'Are we on schedule?' she asked.

'Yes, doing well. But remember, the cashier said there's a gale forecast. When we hit that north coast we'll be in the teeth of it and I'll have to drive more slowly.'

She risked looking at him and felt an instant pang of sympathy. 'You really are whacked, aren't you?'

Her expression softened. He seemed very defenceless. The strong wind had tousled his hair boyishly, the effect enhanced by a lock of hair which fell onto his forehead. Since sitting down, he'd eased his bisecting tie and loosened the top button of his shirt. He looked more approachable than ever.

Their eyes met. Inexplicably his widened, a liquid tenderness appearing in their depths. For a moment Laura could hardly breathe, trapped by the lazy friendship he was projecting. And then she had fiercely snapped her lids down and was jabbing a chip into the sauce on her plate.

The diversion didn't help her trembling knees. They'd developed a life of their own, she thought gloomily.

Max's elbows appeared on the table. She felt the drift of his breath on her forehead.

'What happened to us, Laura?' he asked quietly.

'You went to France, I went to London,' she replied, taking his remark at face value.

She hated him for choosing that particular moment to open old wounds. Service stations weren't ideal places to discuss heartbreak. She scooped up a reckless amount of spicy sauce and concentrated on eating. Something volcanic hit the back of her throat, bringing tears to her eyes.

Max misinterpreted this and caught one of her hands earnestly in both of his.

'Were you mad with me for going to France?' he persisted. 'I never understood what happened. We'd parted as lovers,' he added in reproach.

Tears blurred her eyes. She wasn't sure which were sauce induced and which were genuine, only that she felt upset, and wished he'd never tried to unravel the past.

'Laura!'

His concerned face swam before her. In her blindness, she could have believed that he was shaken…touched by her distress. All the signs were there. But signs could lead you astray.

Laura reached out uncertainly, desperate for a drink. Apparently Max thought that the hand was for him, and he gathered it to his chest like a trophy.

The comfort was too welcome. She had to do something drastic. Already she was wishing he really cared about her. She knew that would be rushing to her own destruction—and only lemmings were *that* dumb.

Angry with herself for succumbing, however briefly, she reclaimed her hand, swept it across her eyes and found a rueful grin from somewhere.

'Save your sympathy for the deserving! I'm not cracking up. It's this gunk!' she accused, poking at the dark sauce on her plate. 'It's murdering my tonsils!'

That had the required effect. Max sat back in his seat as if she'd doused him with cold water. It was the way to treat him if she wanted to stay unaffected by his winsome charm, she realised.

'Drink your coffee,' Max muttered. There were a few moments of silence before he spoke again. 'I was trying to establish what happened. I thought we ought to clear the air, then we could be civil to one another for the next day or so. If you don't want to communicate—'

'I don't. I'd rather steer clear of discussing our past relationship,' she broke in, stiff with tension.

'Generalities, then.' He contemplated her for a moment. 'What did you do when you left Port Isaac and reached London?'

She caught her breath. *I almost died.* 'I took a catering course,' she said instead, concise and clipped with the effort of containing the bitter pain.

Max frowned. 'I thought you loved the village. You told me you never wanted to leave.'

'Woman's privilege,' she said with a shrug of her small shoulders.

'I agree; you've changed your mind with the best of them,' he noted sardonically. 'Still, I found it surprising at the time that you'd gone off to London on your own.'

'Maybe,' she said with an offhand, shallow little laugh, 'the idea of you flying off to Paris gave me the notion that I, too, could spread my wings.'

There was another long silence. Laura ate her ham roll even though she felt it was likely to choke her. Being with Max for hour after hour was stretching her nerves to breaking point. She hoped she could last the course.

Aware that he'd become very still, she found that his attention had been caught by someone just out of her eye line. Turning, she registered the young man fitting

a cute baby into a high chair, and she hastily swung back
again to concentrate on her roll.

'Tell me…'

Laura looked up enquiringly. But Max wasn't ad-
dressing her. He was leaning forwards, speaking to the
young man behind her. She kept her eyes resolutely
fixed on the table in front of her.

'How old is that baby?' Max finished.

'Eight months,' said her father proudly. 'Cracker, isn't
she?'

'A cracker,' agreed Max. He thought for a moment.
'What's she going to eat?'

'You'll know in a minute.' The young man chuckled.
'It'll come flying in your direction.'

Max eyed the baby warily. 'You on your own?' he
asked, a note of awe in his voice.

'Wife's up visiting her sister. Lucy and me are on our
way back from seeing the shire horse centre.'

Laura could see that Max was absorbing everything
that was said to him, as if he was trying to compile a
do-it-yourself manual for babies. Sourly she hoped he
wouldn't interrogate every parent he came across.

'Does she sleep a lot?'

The young man laughed. 'Not enough for me and my
wife to live a normal life! What's the interest? Hey!' he
cried happily. 'Are you and…your…er…expecting…?'

A bolt of pain shot straight through Laura. How dared
Max get cosy and exchange father-talk with total strangers? She flashed a ferocious look at Max, who was
smiling enigmatically and holding up a coy hand as if
the 'good news' hadn't yet been announced.

'Put him straight!' she hissed, deeply hurt.

'He's happy with his assumption. Why disillusion
him?' he whispered.

He had the gall to touch her cheek teasingly, as if

they were lovers. Her stomach churned. 'Because it's not true and never will be!' she ground out.

'Who knows what the future holds?' he asked. 'Laura,' he said, his eyes intense and as dark as shadowed seas, 'we may find that back in our familiar haunts, released from our current responsibilities—'

'No!' she cried in panic. So *that* was what he'd been planning! 'Forget it! We're not taking up where we left off—'

'There are things left unsaid.'

His hand toyed with her hair, and she pulled back irritably, wincing because he didn't let go of the thick, glossy hank he'd captured. Inexorably she was drawn gently forwards again—like a dog on a rope, she thought furiously.

'Because they're not worth saying!' she declared.

'I want answers. I put such a lot in my letters. Why did you ignore them?'

Laura's eyes widened. Fay and her mother hadn't said anything about letters. She felt a pang of longing. They'd probably meant well, but she would have liked to read for herself his explanation of why he had dumped her.

A girl came up and started clearing away the dishes and wiping the table. She did it very slowly, with several smiles for Max, who gave her a quick, 'Thank you', but otherwise continued to watch Laura's dismayed face.

She was becoming very agitated. He was pushing for information and he would go on and on until he'd forced her to relive the agonies she'd suffered.

No. Once was enough.

'Well, Laura?' he probed.

'I was busy,' she snapped, avoiding the whole issue.

Her eyes closed. She felt the blood drain from her face. Busy listening for the sign of any movement in her womb. Busy fighting to stay alive. Coming to terms with her double…triple loss. Max, the baby, her dreams.

'Doing what?'

Her eyes shot open in anger. 'Having fun. Didn't Fay tell you, during one of your long chats together?'

Now admit your affair! Confess your inability to stand anywhere near an attractive woman without seducing her!

'I think,' he drawled, 'Fay was rather preoccupied with something else.'

The barb sliced through her body and made her feel sick. Sure.

Fay had been making a baby with him.

Suddenly she couldn't stand any more. Laura slid out of the seat, grimly averting her eyes from little Lucy and her father. She stalked out, and her heart physically ached as she stormed through the busy concourse towards the main doors.

God, she hurt! Max was twisting her up inside, scraping her raw. There would be nothing left of her by the time she was back in London. The hours ahead terrified her. She couldn't cope. She took in a long, shuddering breath, her eyes wide with panic because she knew she had to stick it out.

And didn't know how.

Almost hysterical with desperation, she flung open the swing door. Adding to her mood with its biting brutality, the wind hit her full on, spinning her around and threatening to lift her off her feet. Setting her jaw, she bent her head and fought it, just as she was fighting her inner emotions.

Ominously, she was no match for the strong wind. She found herself being driven backwards. Close to tears of sheer frustration, she tried to force herself forwards again and was blown sideways. Recognising that she was too lightweight to make headway, she used her brain instead and changed tactic.

To her satisfaction, it worked. Maybe she looked stupid, hauling herself along by hanging onto one parked car after another, her breath catching in her throat, but she got to her destination nevertheless.

Exhausted but grimly triumphant, she embraced the bonnet of the Range Rover like a long-lost lover, and hung on, waiting for Max to appear.

It was a while before a familiar arm came around her. She resisted it.

'Surrender to the inevitable! Throw caution to the wind!' yelled Max.

On a good day she would have giggled. This wasn't a good day by any stretch of the imagination. But, immensely relieved he was there, she let him pull her into the warmth and security of his strong body, burrowing into his chest to shelter from the viciously cutting wind.

He shepherded her to the passenger side of the car, protecting her in the circle of his arms. Yet even he had to struggle—and became involved in a wrestling match to stop the door from being ripped off its hinges.

After a moment he too flung himself into his seat and cocooned them both in safety. A paper napkin was dropped into her lap.

'You forgot your strawberry tart.' He smiled at her cheerfully.

She felt so upset that her instinct was to ram it down his throat. Or crush it in her tense fists and plaster the mess over his smoothie face. But that would alert him to the fact that she was rattled.

'How thoughtful.'

Laura had the shakes. She clutched her trembling hands tightly, incapable of unwrapping the tartlet.

'Are you all right?' he asked, doing it for her.

His lean fingers meshed with hers and she felt the pastry in her hands. She couldn't stop herself from shaking.

'Frightened. I nearly got blown over,' she muttered,

grateful that the gale had given her an excuse to be quivering like a leaf.

'I saw.' He sounded concerned and tender. 'You should have waited for me.'

Laura looked stonily ahead. 'I'd had enough of chatting about the old days.'

'You're as substantial as thistledown. You weren't strong enough to cope on your own,' he said very, very softly.

She tensed. There had been a subtext in that. Were they talking about the same thing? Her heart thudded. What did he know? Fay had sworn she would never tell Max that Laura had miscarried his baby. But...

Fiercely she dismissed the idea that Max knew anything. He'd have been different towards her. Wouldn't he?

'I managed!' she jerked out.

'Just,' he conceded. 'I think you would have done better with me, though, don't you?'

'Are you having this sleep or not?' she flung, changing the subject. The warmth of his satiny voice, flowing through her nerves and magically unknotting them, was getting too much for her.

'Not.' He started the engine. 'The gale is increasing in strength.'

An enigmatic smile curled his lips. She caught a brief but revealing gleam in his eyes. *He was up to something!*

'I don't mind if you take a break,' she said, sounding panicky. At that moment she'd do anything to delay their arrival. 'Please,' she added, nervously turning to face him.

He was watching her closely. There was a long silence while he examined her anxious, pained eyes. With slow deliberation he took in her slightly parted mouth and focused on the gleaming tips of her pearly teeth before letting his gaze sweep down to observe the way her breath shortened and gathered in her slender throat.

The heat coming from his strong, lithe body seemed to increase. Laura swallowed, feeling overwrought and anxious about his intentions. He could destroy her with a few words. She prayed to God that he never discovered what those words were.

The trick was making sure he never came close to thinking she might want to hear them.

'It'll be all right,' he soothed, and she wasn't sure what he meant because she felt so muddled and upset. He gave her a gloriously sunny smile and patted her cold, trembling hand. 'We're moving on while we can.' The smile broadened. 'I think we've made excellent headway so far, don't you?'

They hadn't spoken after that. She'd chewed over and over what he'd said, trying to make sense of it, and Max had been totally tuned in to driving. The radio warned of storm-force gales in the West Country, increasing in strength by the evening.

They had been aware of the strong winds on the journey. Several times Max had wrestled with the steering when they were blown slightly sideways, and Fred had begun to squawk in protest. Laura had jammed his cage more securely between their two cases and talked to him reassuringly till he dozed off again, lulled by the motion.

Now however, when they finally crested the hill above Port Gaverne, neither of them was prepared for the sight before them.

'Wow!' Impressed, Max drew the car to a halt.

'Oh, Max!'

Wide-eyed, Laura stared at the angry sea. It was a dark, dirty grey and was flinging itself at the high black cliffs with such ferocity that spray was flying over the top. At the end of the Main—the narrow spit of land below them—the sea was drowning the eighty-foot Castle Rock in a waterfall of white.

Globules of foam, like giant snowballs, were being blown horizontally for three hundred yards or so across the headland. Somewhere in the distance, thunder was rumbling almost continuously.

'Incredible! I've never seen it like this!' exclaimed Max in awe as the car was battered and shaken by shrieking gusts of wind.

'I have. Once. Well, almost as bad...' Her voice broke. On a day like this, her father had gone out on a lifeboat shout and had never returned.

He took one look at her pale, frozen face and curved a comfortingly big hand around hers. 'When your father died?' he guessed shrewdly.

She nodded, huge misty eyes fixed on the terrible seas, wondering if the lifeboat would have to go out this time. 'I hope everyone's laid up in port,' she said, her voice so thin and reedy that it was drowned by the howling gale and Max had to lean nearer to hear. 'It would be awful to be out there today.'

'Foul.' He gave her hand a sympathetic squeeze. 'Your father was one hell of a man. We all admired him.'

'Did you?' she asked in shy pleasure, turning her head.

He was very close; their faces were almost touching. She searched his face and saw only compassion. Her eyes lingered on the smoothness of his skin, the strength of his jaw...and then the softness of his voice as he said, 'I envied you.'

She blanched, her pupils pinpointing in shock. 'For losing him?'

'No, no!' he cried, his expression passionate in denial, his hands gripping hers hard. 'It's difficult to explain... You had something you could never lose. A father you could look up to and think fondly of for the rest of your life. How old were you?'

'Eleven.'

His eyes darkened like molten tar. 'I was seventeen, on a brief visit home from school. I've never forgotten that winter. Your father's death affected the whole of Port Isaac. People talked of nothing else—how decent a man he was, what a good father he'd been... No one had a bad word to say about him.'

Laura gave a sad little smile, oddly comforted by the memory. 'He was wonderful,' she said, her eyes shining with love and tears. 'Funny, loyal... He loved us so much.'

They were both silent for a while. Perhaps he was remembering how she'd chattered on about her father when she and Max had once wandered along the coast together. The time her father had dressed up as a Chinese magician and awed them all with the tricks he'd been practising for months, then her cry of gleeful recognition when his long, trailing moustache had become dislodged by the flags of all nations emerging from his mouth. The treasure hunts he'd organised... Laura's mouth wobbled. So many lovely memories. Such a loving man.

'I wondered,' said Max quietly, as if far away, 'if anyone would ever remember me with such admiration or if I could earn loyalty and devotion like that. The reaction of the whole village to his death was an extraordinary tribute. It affected me strongly.'

'M-mother was touched by the turn-out at the f-funeral,' she stumbled, amazed that Max could express these thoughts. Why hadn't he said all of this when they had been going out together? He'd been silent. And when she'd urged him to talk about his childhood somehow he'd steered the conversation away.

'I remember...' Max paused, his mouth thinning, then

he plunged on. 'I asked my father why he hadn't ever volunteered for lifeboat duty.'

'And?'

She tensed in anticipation. He'd never spoken of his father before, either. General William Pendennis had been off-limits and she'd never known why. There was so much she didn't know about Max, she realised. Too many secrets for them ever to have been truly close.

'He said that he had more sense than to risk his life for total strangers.'

'Max!'

He gave a humourless laugh at Laura's shocked face. For her, it was inconceivable that anyone might not accept the unwritten law of the sea: that you risked sacrificing your life to save others because the sea was all-powerful and forced everyone concerned with it into a tight-knit band of comradeship. Because one day someone might do the same for you.

'Not exactly well-endowed with humanity, my father,' he said drily. There was a bleakness behind his eyes which belied his offhand delivery. 'We had a violent row after that and we've barely exchanged a civil word since.'

Max played absently with her fingers, but she could see that he was upset. Yet his version of his father didn't tally with what she knew—a man who was upright and caring and appalled at his son's two-timing.

Now she felt confused. She shared the values Max was describing. His father sounded selfish and heartless. But she knew Max could be both those things too. So what was she to believe?

'We all envied *you*,' she said, hoping to learn a little more. 'You seemed to have everything.'

'Not anything I wanted.' His hands were still now, resting lightly on hers. 'We were what the Americans would call dysfunctional. I've always wanted to be part of a close family group. As you said, wife, two point four children.'

Laura was quiet for a moment. The fiancée had obviously not liked Max's fling with Fay and the relationship had foundered. 'I thought you must be married by now,' she said slowly. 'You must have had plenty of opportunities.'

His eyes flickered with hard lights. 'Plenty. Never found the right woman, though. You always want what you can't have, don't you?'

Laura couldn't speak. She'd believed that Max had never been serious about his relationships. Now he was telling her that he'd been eager for commitment but his girlfriends hadn't matched up to his ideals. That included her, of course—but she'd known that.

It was a new angle on him. A would-be family man. But...was he being sincere? Gazing out at the nightmare seas, she decided it didn't matter because it didn't concern her at all. He'd rejected her once already as marriageable material—and even if he was interested, which he wasn't, she'd be a waste of his time.

Max wanted children.

Oh, God! she thought bleakly. It hurt her to think of him some time in the future, beaming around his breakfast table at a beautiful wife and his dark-eyed, vibrant toddlers and babies!

Not, she hastily told herself, because she loved him, but because it was an experience she'd never know herself. And it was to some extent his fault.

But Fay was fecund. Fay was wonderful fun, and stunning to look at. Max had fallen at Fay's feet. Yet she had dumped Max for Daniel—and maybe, despite his bitter denials, Max was still hankering after her. Hate was so close to love, they said. Perhaps Max was covering up his disappointment by disparaging Fay.

What would he do when he discovered that he was

almost halfway to his desired family? There was already one child who properly belonged to him.

Laura knew a moment of pure panic. He was about to see his son…and surely he'd fall in love with Perran and be loath to let him go? Her mind raced on, seeing Max visiting, playing the uncle…until he or Daniel guessed—or Fay told him the truth. And Max would want his son.

She went icy cold.

Max rubbed her clammy, trembling hands. 'Let's get in the warm. I have to admit, I'm looking forward to practising parenthood, aren't you?'

'No!' she said wretchedly.

'Don't believe you!' he teased. 'All women are nuts about kids.'

'Children!'

'What?'

'Call them children! Kids…it's casual. Uncaring. Off-hand.'

'Whatever you like,' he said breezily. 'All set?'

Laura drove her nails into her hands, steeling herself for the meeting, feeling sicker and sicker by the minute.

For a short time they were sheltered from the gale by the depth of the steep, narrow lane which led to the beach. It had been cut into the rock long ago, by Dartmoor convicts, for horse-drawn carts carrying slate. Laura could see even now the marks on the rock walls where the carts had run the hubs of their wheels to slow down.

There was the path leading to the tiny rock-ledge quay. Soon they'd reach the beach, where masted ships had once been loaded up by women stevedores.

But not in weather like this.

They had reached the bottom of the lane and were now at the head of the cove, facing head-on the full mercy of the gale as it ripped down the narrow inlet and shook the high-bodied car unmercifully.

Fred began to make funny little noises of desperation. But Laura was too stunned to pay him any heed.

The beach and half the sandy bay and its rocks were uncovered, though the tide was coming in. The neck of the cove was filled with boiling, rolling white surf, each roller thirty, forty, fifty feet high, she estimated, and crashing down with a deafening thunder. That was the noise they'd heard a few moments ago.

'It's an incredible sight,' breathed Max, his face alight with excitement.

She looked up at the little cottage dug into the side of the cliff. 'I hope Perran isn't scared!'

'More likely thrilled, if he's got any Pendennis nerve in him.'

'Fay mentioned that Perran was a bit of a toughie,' she conceded nervously.

By all accounts her nephew was bold and daring, like Max—and totally unlike Daniel. Laura knew Max would be surprised at Perran's boisterous nature, when his brother was so lethargic and vague.

With a smile to reassure her, Max slowly swung the car up the small hill, past the fish cellars and the old lime kiln.

Laura licked her lips. The cottage looked smaller than she remembered. They'd be horribly on top of one another. Two children and Max, stuck indoors because of the vile weather... She clenched her jaw. It didn't bear thinking about.

Fear clamoured in her dry throat and made her body limp. Fred was now screeching at the top of his voice, driving her crazy. She wanted to open the car door and tumble out, then run and run till she was exhausted—but far away from Max and the children and all the baggage that came with the situation.

He drew up outside the cottage. 'Shut up, Fred!' he bellowed. The parrot stopped in mid-squawk. Laura was impressed. Max seemed to think nothing of it. 'I'll announce our arrival,' he said with a gentleness that crept in under her defences and weakened her still further. 'Stay where you are till I come and get you.' He wriggled into his waxed coat. 'That's an order. You'd get blown over the cliff if you tried to make it on your own.'

He could barely open the door. Gritting his teeth, cursing the wind, he heaved it open and slid out.

The gale caught his hair and plastered it flat against his head, then, as he turned to the cottage, hanging onto the car all the while, it whipped every strand across his face so that he could hardly see where he was going.

Laura watched him in alarm, straining anxiously on the edge of her seat as he fought his way to the little plank front door and banged on the knocker.

The door opened. Max disappeared, only to reappear a moment or two later. Hurrying towards her, he motioned to her to lower the window a little.

'I'll...get...you...in!' he yelled, the wind snatching his breath away. 'Leave...me...to unload.'

'Fred!' she cried, frightened that her beloved pet would never survive the battering he'd get.

Max thrust his head deeper inside. She saw that his face was glistening with spray. 'I'll look after him,' he promised. 'Throw a coat over the cage or something. I promise. I know he means a lot to you. Now, close the window and be ready.'

The dreaded moment had come. She felt the pulsing of fear as she zipped up her long jacket and tied its hood tightly. She scooped up as many loose items as she could carry to save Max too many journeys, and nodded at him. Even he was near to being blown off his feet, and he was having difficulty keeping his balance.

His arms embraced her, his body protected her once

more. Even so, her stockinged legs were soaked in seconds. With Laura tucked against his chest, Max staggered towards the small cottage door.

Laura couldn't breathe. The wind sliced under her hood and ripped it from her head. Stinging salt spray lashed her face and tugged at her wildly whipping hair. Gasping for air, buffeted by the greedy wind and almost blinded, she suddenly found herself surrounded by a relative calm.

'OK?' He held her against him still and she stayed there, wet, breathless and secure.

She didn't want him to go. Scared of meeting the children, she tried to delay him and said, her voice shaking, 'Just getting my breath back!'

His hold on her tightened. 'Don't worry,' he assured her quietly. 'You'll do fine. Trust me.'

He'd gone before she could respond. Trust. It all came down to that in the end. She had learnt to her cost what he was like beneath that desirable exterior. And he wasn't the kind of man she could entrust with her hopes and fears and ambitions, let alone her temporary friendship.

'You Laura?'

A young woman was standing at the end of the passage, her hair adorned with beads and straggling ribbons, her clothes long, black and droopy, a scowl on her thin grey features.

'Yes. I'm Laura.'

Max returned with a huge box in his arms and disappeared again. Laura couldn't move it, so she left it alone.

Fay's friend seemed disinclined to help. 'Baby's upstairs asleep. *He's* in there...' There was a jerk of a grimy thumb. 'And the best of bloody luck. I've called a taxi.'

'Sorry?' Laura unzipped her jacket and shook water from her hair, trying to make sense of all that.

Max lurched in with their bags and then hurried out.

'I'm going,' said the woman.

'Now?' Laura gasped.

With a tightening of her pinched mouth, the woman eyed Laura wearily. 'There isn't room for you two and me.'

Laura went white. 'But...' She gulped as her stomach swooped with alarm. 'We don't know anything about children! You have to run through their routine!'

'Routine?' Fay's friend looked as though Laura had accused her of child molesting. 'Are you joking?'

Appalled, Laura was about to ask a few questions when the door crashed open again, revealing Max clutching a huge bundle carefully in his arms.

'Fred!' she cried, feverishly unwrapping the waxed coat from the cage.

'He's OK. I can hear him swearing at me,' Max said in amusement.

A thought struck her, and she looked up. Max was wearing only his suit. Some time during the dash from the car his jacket had come undone and his shirt was soaked, plastered to his toned torso like clingfilm. Before she could stop herself, she reached out and exploratively touched his chest with the tips of her dainty fingers.

'You're wet through!' she protested. 'Shivering!'

He reacted with ridiculous pleasure, beaming all over his face as if she'd said something meaningful. His hand waved in the air carelessly.

'I'll warm up.'

She bit back the urge to send him up to change into something warm. It would sound too wifely.

'I'm afraid your suit will be ruined from the salt spray. You did this for Fred!' Her expression softened with gratitude.

'No.' He gave her a cock-eyed grin. 'For you. It's obvious you dote on the scrawny little oddball.'

'Thank you,' she said simply, and he held her warm gaze for a breathtaking length of time.

'Right. I'm off.' Responding to the hooting of a car outside, Fay's friend manoeuvred around them, a rucksack on her back. She had banged in and out of the door before Max had gathered his wits together.

'Dammit, what's she doing?' He seemed furious with everyone, including Laura, as if it was her fault that he'd been slow off the mark.

'It's too late, Max.' The butterflies were darting about in her stomach again. 'She's gone. We have to do this on our own.'

'Why?' he demanded, bewildered.

Laura drew in a sharp breath. 'She said…there wasn't room for all of us.'

She eyed the cramped passageway and narrow stairs apprehensively. How many bedrooms would there be? Let there be enough, she prayed.

He seemed stunned. 'Of all the…' His eyes flashed with black anger. 'So much for the intro! Of all the feckless, selfish… God! Words fail me! I'm going to wring your sister's neck when I get to her!'

'Do Daniel's for me, will you?' she muttered, irritated that everything always had to be Fay's fault. She felt strangely deflated. The lovely moment of friendship had gone. She doubted it would be revived again. 'We…we'd better check on the children,' she ventured. 'The baby's upstairs. Would you go? I'll head for Perran. He's somewhere back there.'

But she was reluctant to move. Her mouth had gone dry. She was about to put her emotions on the line. A shudder ran the whole length of her body.

'Come on. You need a cup of tea inside you. Not bothered by this, are you? At least Perran won't bite.'

That's what you think! she said to herself. Laura drew herself erect. 'Tea sounds wonderful,' she called as he hurried up the stairs. 'I'll make it. Don't be long.'

Plucking up all her courage, she persuaded her unwilling legs to start moving towards the room at the end of the passage.

CHAPTER FOUR

LAURA found herself looking into a small kitchen. Thankfully it had been modernised for the holiday market, but it didn't look very clean.

Perran was sitting at a pine table which was covered in oilcloth. He'd been eating baked beans and sausages—rather inaccurately, judging by the mess around his mouth.

She gripped the doorframe for support. He had Max's black hair, Max's molten brown eyes and endless lashes, Max's honeyed colouring. Max's scowl.

'Baby's fast asleep and, yes, I checked that she was breathing,' came Max's voice from behind her.

Nervously she jerked her head around to see if Max was as dumbstruck as she was. In fact he seemed more concerned with the disorderly kitchen, and she breathed a sigh of relief. Then her nerves began to jangle as she wondered how long it would be before he picked up on the extraordinary likeness.

'Hello!' Laura said uncertainly, feeling awkward and out of place in her city suit. She wished she'd thought this through and opted for an old jumper and jeans, Max or no Max.

Perran clearly didn't like what he saw either. He looked back at her with all the enthusiasm of a carved stone cherub. Laura shifted uneasily. It wasn't the welcome she'd been expecting.

'Try again,' muttered Max, his mouth somewhere near her right ear.

Momentarily distracted by the warm flow of Max's breath, she dragged her attention back to Perran. And suddenly it dawned on her that the little boy must be scared of the two strangers who'd popped up from nowhere, looking as though they'd come to do a business deal with the head of some corporation.

Putting aside her own fears, she gave him a big, beaming smile and walked into the room.

'You're *much* bigger than I thought!' The flattery didn't warrant even a blink. Laura tried a different tack. 'I'm your Aunty Laura, and this is Uncle Max. You remember I sent you a cattle truck and a hay barn for your birthday?'

Perran's eyes flickered imperceptibly in recognition but otherwise there was no response. Laura's compassionate smile warmed her eyes. He had such a sweet little mouth, she thought dreamily.

'Hi,' said Max in a low growl, and Perran and Laura jumped.

Again her eyes slanted sideways to watch for any sign of recognition, any hint in Max's voice that some intangible thread of common genes was drawing him to his son—and to the inevitable conclusion.

But Max was just Max, standing relaxed and totally at ease, a direct, pleasant smile on his face. Her legs became a little unsteady again and she leaned on a chair, her pulses hammering violently.

'Mummy's friend's had to go out,' she explained, when Perran remained silent. 'We've come to look after you till Mummy comes back.'

Her nephew still didn't respond. Laura's heart went out to him. He must be missing his mother dreadfully. Her fists clenched. She could gladly give Fay a piece of her mind! Poor little mite.

'Hug him, or something,' said Max, out of the corner of his mouth.

'*You* hug him!' she whispered, taut with nerves. She stared at Perran helplessly, yearning to hold his sweet little body, terrified that she'd bawl her eyes out when she did.

'I think we must look a bit wild,' Max murmured.

Laura nodded. Max had a wonderful, rumpled appearance. She put up a tentative hand to her own hair and felt the tendrils glued together with sticky salt. She must be a total mess.

When Max took a step forward, Perran calmly picked up a bean-encrusted spoon and began to flick food around the kitchen.

'Stop that!' snapped Max. Three sauce-coated beans were sliding down his right temple. Laura stifled a nervous giggle then held her breath at the affront to his dignity. 'Stop it *at once!*' he said, lowering his voice to a menacing growl.

'*Max!*' she hissed as Perran's hand faltered and his eyes widened warily.

'He's issued a challenge,' Max muttered, staring Perran down. 'And I'm establishing who's the leader of the pack.'

'He's not a dog!'

'Near enough. I think children and dogs need the same things. Food, water, shelter, endless love, attention and no contradictory behaviour to confuse them. Simple, rock-steady rules.'

She gave Max a withering glance. What did he know about children?

'You can't be that inflexible.'

'One will over another. Establish who's the boss, what the parameters are. *Then* you can be flexible. See what I mean?' he said, still holding Perran with his uncompromising gaze.

The spoon was being lowered. So were Perran's eyes. His lower lip quivered, and Laura could bear it no more. With a cry of sympathy, she rushed forward and enveloped him in her arms, stroking the little boy's stiff back and hoping Max hadn't frightened him irreversibly.

She shook with longing. Despite the beans and a sour smell of milk, he was everything she'd dreamed of. Jet-black curls crept around a dinky, shell-shaped—and rather dirty—ear. He had such a little body and she felt terribly protective. Her heart swooped with love.

'It's OK,' she said soothingly, kissing the top of his head. 'No one's going to hurt you. We'll take care of you. We'll have a lot of fun.'

She smiled sentimentally into his sullen face. He remained quite unmoving and unmoved, like a wooden doll. Horribly conscious that she was trespassing, she released her hold, feeling stupid and rejected. And she was more upset than she could have imagined. Her whole body trembled, from head to foot. She'd loved that moment. He'd hated it. She was shocked.

'Perran, you won't ever throw food about again!' warned Max, still with his Godzilla stare. The little boy stuck his hands on his non-existent hips belligerently and fixed his cold, dark eyes on Max's wet-stained stomach. 'War's been declared,' Max observed under his breath.

'Oh, no, Max! He's a little boy!' she protested.

'Spoilt.'

'Confused.'

'Indulged,' growled Max.

The air fizzed with the mutual hatred between Max and Perran. Laura felt dismayed that they had got off on the wrong foot. This wasn't what she'd imagined at all. It was ironic that she'd been worried about how she would react when faced with two children who would demand her love. It was quite possible they'd never get that far!

A wet cloth was dumped on the table. 'OK, pardner. You round up the runaway critters here; I'll chase any strays elsewhere.'

Max was issuing his own challenge—and, amazingly, the silent Perran seemed to understand it because he began clumsily wiping up the splattered food.

'How—?' began Laura in amazement.

'Cowboy films,' Max muttered in a quiet aside. 'Took a bet that he watched them.'

Defeated, she put on the kettle and made a pot of tea, helpfully pointing out dripping beans and stray sausage to Max. His psychology might be cock-eyed, but it had worked. And she—she'd been a total failure.

It seemed her maternal intuitions had been lost along with her ability to bear children. Miserably, she poured out the tea, and, seeing Perran looking wistfully at her mug, made him a weak cup too.

They both sat glumly at the table, listening to the howling gale outside and watching the tousled Max prowling around in his usual restless way, capturing the odd sliding bean or two and fingering surfaces critically.

'This place is filthy,' he said in disgust. 'I doubt this is the first time the contents of Perran's plate have gone AWOL. We've got to get the children out of here, Laura, first thing in the morning. Get somewhere decent and inculcate decent standards.'

Wincing at the thought of somewhere lined throughout in stainless steel and hosed down with disinfectant every day, she fetched a wet teatowel and wiped her nephew's mucky face and hands and firmly dried them, despite his screwed up eyes and mouth routine. She wanted to discuss what Max had said, but could see Perran casting a mischievous and calculating eye over her mug of tea and she wanted to divert him.

'I'm going to put my parrot on his perch,' she announced casually. Pleased at Perran's guarded interest, she held out her hand. 'Coming?'

He glowered and put his hands behind his back. Laura

gave an 'I don't care' shrug, turned her back on him and left the kitchen, calling unnecessarily, 'Fred, Fred!'

She heard Max's feet on the stairs again; he was presumably checking on Kerenza. When he wandered into the tiny front room a few moments later, a mug of tea in his hand, she was settling Fred on his high perch and Perran was watching, silent but attentive.

'Water,' she said, holding out Fred's container in Perran's direction. She took great care not to look at her nephew and was relieved when the container was snatched from her hand and the little boy ran from the room.

'He'll come round,' said Max confidently, when Laura looked at him with a worried frown on her face. 'I've seen kids like this before—'

'When?' she asked, her heart thumping. He wasn't married...but could he have first-hand knowledge after all? She was shocked that she felt so desolate.

Max came closer and absently rubbed her arm in friendly reassurance. 'I'm a financier,' he reminded her. 'I have a clutch of day nurseries I put up money for. Occasionally I visit.'

'Oh.' She felt mollified. An extraordinary relief had accompanied his explanation. 'Like...you get down on your knees and play with them?'

Max tried to look casual. 'Something of the sort. I have a manager in charge of the nurseries, of course. We discuss guidelines for staff and parents.'

At least one of them had some vague idea of what to do. 'That'll be helpful,' she mumbled, inexplicably floored by the image of Max larking about with toddlers.

'You're finding this hard, aren't you?' he mused shrewdly.

'I—I never thought that Perran would be difficult, or so wary of us,' she admitted. 'I'd imagined...'

She took a deep breath. His hand was still now, his

eyes gentle and understanding. She hadn't expected that, either.

'You thought we'd be one happy family?'

Laura went red and she moved away, making much of filling Fred's seed tin then emptying it again because she wanted Perran to do that little job.

They both jumped when the window rattled. Max went to wedge it. The wind was even stronger than before. It clawed and snatched in rapacious gusts at the little window, and Laura was glad that the cottage was so sturdy and had survived countless storms like this over the last two hundred years.

'I thought,' she said almost normally, grateful for that interlude to gather herself together, 'you and I would be at each other's throats and the children would be clinging to—to—'

'You. And you'd be acting like a mother hen while I pushed off and only came back to be fed,' he finished for her.

'Something like that,' she mumbled.

Logically, it would suit her if Perran kept his distance. But she didn't want that. She wanted him to love her. How muddle-headed could she *get*?

'I intend to be fully involved in this,' Max said quietly. 'I think this is an opportunity for both of us to learn something.'

'The art of nappy-changing?' she suggested, using flippancy to hide her hurt.

He confounded her with an enigmatic smile. 'Here's your water-bearer. While you've got him occupied, I'll take our stuff upstairs, have a bath, change and keep an eye on Kerenza now and then in case she wakes up. I'm loath to leave you, but I don't want to catch pneumonia.'

Filled with guilt, she nodded, even though she felt panic-stricken at being left alone with Perran. She decided she needed a good shake. It was idiotic to be alarmed at the company of a child.

'You do that,' she said bravely. 'Don't…don't be too long, though.' Max gave a weary nod and she felt even more of a heel. 'Forgive me,' she said apologetically. 'I'd forgotten you've just driven a few hundred miles on top of a tiring journey. I'm being selfish. We'll be up in a while. It must be nearly Perran's bathtime.'

'We'll attack him together.' He smiled at her lazily.

'Poor little scrap!' she said, with a breathless little laugh. It was a bit ragged at the edges; she had in her mind's eye the two of them bathing his son. Something about that scenario made the air catch in her throat and the colour drain from her face.

Clumsily she pulled a chair near to Fred's perch so that Perran could reach it and clip on the water pot.

'When we're on our own,' mused Max, 'we'll have to talk child-care tactics.'

He took her shaking hand in his and held it tightly. Her lip trembled. His voice was low and husky and it was in danger of making her go weak at the knees.

'Oh, Max!' she cried, managing a dismissive laugh. 'This isn't some takeover campaign! We're dealing with a little boy—'

'And we have to do this properly.'

'But we're not staying long.'

'That doesn't make any difference. I don't believe in compromising my principles.'

Laura looked at him aghast. 'Let's not make this harder for ourselves than it is! We don't know what we're doing. It's not our business to interfere in the way Perran's been brought up—'

Max's grunt interrupted her. 'Dragged.'

'Oh, go and play with your plastic duck!' she snapped.

He smiled faintly. 'I knew I'd forgotten something.'

Max made a dignified exit.

Laura sank to her knees and watched disconsolately as Perran filled the seed pot. After several attempts to fix it in place on the end of the perch, and after a shower of seed had planted itself in Laura's hair, it was finally clipped in correctly. The little boy clambered off the chair and looked back at his handiwork with undisguised pleasure.

Fred danced. Joyous smiles lit Perran's face, and he danced too, encouraging Fred all the more.

Laura felt thrilled. She ached to take Perran in her arms and hold him close. In the increasing gloom, she pressed a hand against her bruised heart and felt it pounding rapidly.

Then she heard Max running down the stairs. Expecting some disaster, she twisted around as he snapped on the light.

Her startled gaze slithered all over him. Slowly. Hungrily.

He'd stripped off his shirt and wore only his trousers. She heard her breath shorten. He looked magnificent—satin-smooth, tanned, firm. Touchable, and potently male.

The muscles of her stomach clenched. With difficulty she met his eyes. They were hooded, as if concealing secrets, but his mouth had become so erotic and kissable that she found her lips softening, as if in preparation.

Somehow she covered up her extraordinary reaction with an acid, 'Now what?'

'I think you ought to know a couple of developments.' His dark voice was rich and low, insinuating itself into every corner of her body. 'You won't like either of them.'

Laura hardly heard. Her pulses began to pound in her ears. The heat was coming off him in waves, bathing her in it as if she stood in front of an oven. Her tongue seemed stuck in her mouth, and she was terrified that he'd notice her confusion...and swoop.

Because she longed to be kissed by that humorous, demanding mouth. Wanted to be held, to run her hands over his impressive shoulders, to feel the hardness of his body against hers.

It was only because she felt vulnerable. Max represented a strength which she did not have at that moment. Laura knew that had to be dealt with. She needed to find some kind of resilience for herself if she was to survive these pseudo-intimate moments. He'd be barging about half-naked morning and night till they sorted out a nanny.

He came to stand in front of her. Bent down, swamping her in the scent of his male body. Touched her head—her foul, tangled, salty head, artfully scattered with an assortment of seeds. Laura knew he was going to make some derogatory remark, and steeled herself for it.

'You do know you have seed in your hair?' he asked, affectionate laughter threading his voice.

She gave a quick glance in the direction of his face, and, perkily as possible, she said, 'I got in the sowing line.'

He chuckled and straightened. 'Then you'd better have the bathroom after me—before you grow a crop of sunflowers and become of commercial interest to agriculture,' he suggested with lazy warmth.

She hid her smile and sighed in genuine pleasure. 'A bath! Warm suds, clean, deseeded hair...sounds wonderful!'

'Yes. Er...about those two problems...'

Laura nodded and tucked her slender legs more firmly under her. His eyelids fluttered as though he was contemplating something carnal. She froze up again.

'Go on,' she prompted cautiously.

Apologetically, he gave a little grimace. 'The first snag is that there are only two bedrooms. One with a double bed.'

He made that sound significant. It might be, to him. 'What's the problem? That's fine for me,' she said, refusing to allow him to make a problem where problems didn't exist.

'Glad one of us is happy,' he said drily. 'So where do I sleep? There isn't a sofa.'

She glanced around the room. Nothing but small cottage chairs—none of them big enough for Max to sleep on. Well, tough! She lifted a determined face.

'You'll have to share with Perran,' she said flatly.

'Ah. Slight problem.'

He didn't look very bothered about the slight problem, and she began to wonder if he *was* hoping that she'd oblige him for the next night or two.

'I thought there might be.' She gazed at him levelly.

With a winning smile and a calculatingly languid look, he pretended to heave a little sigh. 'He's in a tiny half-bed. We *could* double-stack, like a club sandwich, I suppose,' he said helpfully. 'But I think the bed would break beneath my weight.'

Laura scowled. He was finding this funny. It annoyed her to see the laughter lurking behind those insolent dark eyes.

'I'm coming to look. I'm sure we could perch you on the curtain rail or in the bath.' She blinked, disconcerted by his amiable grin. 'Perran,' she went on, extremely nervous about Max's intentions, 'will you be all right for a moment? I'm just going upstairs a minute…' Her voice tailed away. Perran was giving her his dumb, hostile glare again. 'Perran?' She frowned. 'Do you understand? I'm going upstairs. Yes?'

To her surprise, the little boy turned his back on her and set about entertaining Fred.

'Laura...' Suddenly serious, Max pushed a hand through his tangled hair in distraction. 'Perran... There's something important I forgot to tell you. That makes *three* things you won't like,' he corrected, and this time he was genuinely troubled.

Coldly she motioned him out. He stopped to bolt the front door, which had been rattling its latch every time it was caught by each fresh gust of wind.

On the landing at the top of the stairs, she grabbed his arm and confronted him. 'Let's hear the rest, then!'

'Now, don't get mad—'

'Speak!' she hissed.

'All right, all right,' he grumbled unconvincingly. 'Just don't yell at me.'

'Why might I do that?' she asked icily.

He took a deep breath. 'Because I'm cancelling the arrival of the nannies—'

'You're *what*?'

'I have to! Seeing them tomorrow is impractical!'

'Why?' she asked in panic.

'Well, look at the place! We clearly couldn't set up a series of interviews here—not unless they sit on each other's laps while they are waiting!'

Laura gaped in horror. No nannies! The thought was too awful to contemplate. 'But...we could meet them somewhere else—a local hotel, for instance. What about The Headlands, across the bay?'

'And what would we do with the children? There's one hell of a gale blowing out there, if you hadn't noticed, and torrential rain forecast tomorrow. You wouldn't take a dog out in weather like that, let alone two kiddies.'

'We've got the car!'

'You saw what it was like, getting in and out! It would be a nightmare. The Headlands is even more exposed than the road here. Of course, we could leave the children to fend for themselves in the cottage with strict instructions to be good!' he suggested with heavy sarcasm. 'No, Laura. As I said. It isn't practical. We have to leave interviewing for a day or so. I'll tell my secretary first thing tomorrow to hang fire till I contact her again.'

Very convenient. She glared, her blue eyes as hard and glinting as sapphires. 'I'm not staying here with you for more than a couple of days!'

'You may have to. You know what I'll do if you renege on this,' he said under his breath. 'I'd have no qualms about dumping them in care.'

'You're all heart,' she said scornfully, knowing she had to agree. 'But I'll agree to wait till the weather's less horrendous and we can get the children to the hotel without difficulty.' Her mouth firmed. 'As for your bed…we'll rig up something for tonight—chair cushions or whatever; the kitchen table if necessary!—and you can damn well go out and buy a camp bed for yourself tomorrow. That'll concentrate your mind wonderfully on getting a nanny—'

'We'll interview as soon as possible, but I doubt any self-respecting nanny would take the job, once he or she knew they'd have to live here,' he pointed out with infuriating truth. 'We need to find somewhere that's larger and a hell of a lot cleaner.'

Laura felt like screaming. He was absolutely right. Everything was conspiring against her! Murphy's Law, it was called. If something could go wrong, it would.

'That could take weeks!'

'Not the way I operate.'

She felt control slipping away. Problems were multiplying. 'If you delay,' she threatened, 'if you turn down perfectly decent accommodation…'

'I wouldn't dream of it.' He smiled so openly that she

found herself reluctantly believing him. 'Though I'm fascinated to know what you'd do if I did.'

'I'd set Fred on you!'

He clapped a theatrical hand to his forehead, his head flung back in mock agony. 'Anything,' he cried dramatically, while she fought not to be affected by the perfect lines of his throat and jaw. 'Anything but the bald parrot torture!'

Laura gave an irritated sniff and went to inspect the main room—which she'd identified by the size of the bed she'd seen through the open door. Apart from the double bed the furnishings were sparse, with no special little touches to make it homely. She took one look and decided that she'd send Max out the next day to rent a more comfortable holiday home, gale-force winds or not.

She became aware that he was lounging against the doorframe, watching her. 'Baby's in the next room,' he offered.

Laura immediately tensed. So she straightened the grubby pink candlewick bedspread, which looked as though an army had been practising manoeuvres across it.

She was putting off the moment when she and Kerenza would become acquainted. Somehow she knew that would be even harder than facing Perran. And she wanted to be alone in case her feelings got the better of her.

'I won't disturb her,' she said casually.

'Pretty little thing. Blonde. Like Fay and Daniel, not dark at all.'

Laura dropped the pillow she'd been plumping up, and had to work hard not to check out his expression. His voice had been neutral enough, but...

'That's nice. I'd better go back to Perran,' she said hoarsely, moving towards the door. 'You have your bath—'

'Wait.'

She didn't have much choice. He was blocking the exit. She stared, like Perran, at his stomach, then found the acres of gleaming bare skin too intimately displayed and awkwardly bent her tousled head, as if her salt-stained shoes bore a huge fascination for her.

'Now what?' she muttered.

'The third thing I had to tell you.'

Alerted by the new tension in his body, she dragged her gaze slowly up. Lean, strong legs. Narrow hips. That hard, beautiful body... She ended up at his jaw and thought it best to stay there. Being so close to Max seemed to be playing havoc with her pulses. Or perhaps she was scared of what he was about to reveal.

Fay, she thought dully. He does know. He's going to crucify me with the details, explain why Perran is dark—

'It's about Perran,' he said.

The sickness lurched from her stomach to her throat. Tears pricked her eyes.

'Laura,' Max said with a cruel gentleness. 'You're really hung up about something—'

'Yes!' she cried, flinging up her head, allowing him to see the agony in her eyes. 'I am! Now tell me what you want to say and let's be done with it!'

'I don't...' He frowned, saw she was adamant, and took a conceding intake of breath. 'OK. But we'll have to talk—'

'Now!' she seethed, her eyes blazing because she was unable to bear the tension any more. 'Get on with this!'

'I didn't tell you initially because I thought it might upset you.'

She snorted. If he only knew! He couldn't make things much worse. 'Well?'

Max angled his head as though he was deeply moved. That set her teeth on edge. He tried to reach out for her but she moved back with a warning look. His hand fell to his side.

'Have you heard of anything odd about Perran?' he asked softly.

'Like…what?' She was too strung up to say more.

'Anything Fay's said?'

Her whole body went stiff. 'I got the impression that he drives Fay mad,' she offered.

Max had an unnervingly compassionate look in his eyes. 'But she didn't say why, apparently? Perhaps I'm adding this up wrongly, but…' Laura waited without breathing. Here it came. Her eyes implored him to get on with it. 'This friend of Fay's. When we spoke on the phone, she called him a vile brat. There may be a reason for this.'

'Yes. The friend's useless and Perran dislikes her.'

'More worrying than that, I think,' said Max quietly. 'In the two weeks the woman has been caring for him, she claims that he hasn't spoken a word.'

Laura clutched at him in a knee-jerk reaction, her mind racing. It wasn't the awful revelation she'd been expecting. Relief mingled with dismay, turning her bones to jelly, and she hung onto Max with an unwise desperation.

'Oh, poor little scrap!' she cried.

'Maybe I'm wrong,' he said soothingly, stroking her tangled hair. 'It mightn't be anything physical, just psychological.'

She jerked back, still trembling, but wary of letting him sweep her into his pack and 'top dog' it over her. She had to stay independent and cope on her own. And fight the urge to sigh and let Max take charge… He'd do it so well, the idea was horribly tempting. He seemed only too keen to play the traditional fatherly role—but that would make her Mother. She compressed her quivering lips to keep them firm, and clung onto Max's last suggestion.

'Yes…I'm sure it's because Perran's afraid!' she declared, shutting her mind to any other possibility. Fay had said nothing about her nephew having a disability. 'He's been abandoned by his parents and he doesn't understand what's going on!' She wrenched herself free and lowered her voice, conscious that Perran might be listening. 'I'll get him to talk!' she said confidently. 'You see if I don't!'

Max gave her an approving smile. The back of his hand lightly brushed her cheek in an almost affectionate gesture. Laura held onto the shreds of her composure with difficulty, her eyes almost silver with the intensity of her gaze.

'If anyone can get through to him,' Max said, with an admiration that startled her, 'you can. Go and see what you can do. I won't be long in here.' He gestured to the bathroom. 'And you can have your turn while I find Perran's pyjamas and check on Kerenza. Then we'll de-grime the lad and we'll have earned ourselves a stiff drink and supper. How does that sound?'

'Great…' She clenched her jaw. He was stroking her face again. Before he destroyed her will-power entirely, she had to make her position clear. Coolly she swatted his hand away. 'But please don't touch me. This is a difficult situation, and I have no intention of ending up in your bed.'

'How could you?' he murmured innocently. A more believable wicked grin slashed his handsome face. 'I don't have one.'

He disappeared into the bathroom. She was sure from the flexing muscles in his back that he was laughing.

Laura felt wiped out by the growing sexual tension between them. Every move he made, every word he spoke, merely emphasised the highly erotic reaction she had to him. That was all it was—a dreadful, primitive attraction, with no hint of depth to it.

In that case, it would be easy to overcome.

For a split second she felt reassured. Then it occurred to her that he hadn't actually denied her accusation about ending up in his bed. All he'd done was to point out that he didn't have one. But *she* did—a double. That would do him nicely, she thought, biting her lip in agitation.

He was singing again. 'Love Me Tonight'. She took several deep breaths to quell her anger. Gradually her stomach stopped lurching about, her pulses found a rhythm closer to normality.

Max continued crooning at full throttle.

On impulse, she put her mouth to the old-fashioned keyhole and sang a snatch or two of 'Nellie the Elephant', then smugly marched into her bedroom to dig out some clean clothes.

Max's open suitcase was next to hers, on the bed. Before she knew it, she was fingering the tan suede jeans. Her hand stilled. There was a book beneath them. Intrigued to know Max's bedtime reading, she lifted the jeans aside and found herself looking at *Bringing Up Baby*.

Thoughtfully she lifted it out and turned the pages. He *could* have bought it in London before he came to see her. But…if he'd been expecting *her* to take responsibility for the children, why would he want a book like that?

He could have intended to give it to her—in which case, why hadn't he offered it immediately, as a means of persuading her that she could cope perfectly well on her own?

Because, said her suspicious mind, Max had a hidden agenda. A gleam came into Laura's eyes. She'd been to hell and back because of him. This time she was not going to fall for any of his lies.

CHAPTER FIVE

FEELING invigorated after a hasty bath, Laura dressed in jeans and an easy cotton shirt, then wrapped a towel around her newly washed hair. When she emerged from her bedroom, she could hear Max talking to Perran in the bathroom.

'So we'll fill it up really high,' he was saying as she walked barefoot along the landing, 'and you can show me if you can swim or not. Got any bath toys?'

There was no answer. But Laura couldn't recall seeing any, so she ran downstairs and collected a couple of saucepan lids, a colander and a plastic jug and pudding bowls.

'Terraaa!' she announced, bursting into the bathroom with a noisy clatter.

Max stopped trying to wrestle with Perran's jumper and applauded. 'Mine's the colander,' he said enthusiastically. 'Are you a bowl man, or a saucepan man, Perran?'

Apparently neither. Perran's mouth was set in an unsmiling line. Determined to make him break into laughter, Laura hurled her booty into the bath and began to make waves behind the saucepan lids. 'Small one's winning,' she cried. 'Bet that's yours, Perran!'

Max lifted the little boy into the water. He sat there like a lump of wood so Max sabotaged Laura's lids by pouring water on them from a great height. She retaliated, giggling all the while, by squirting some of her bath foam into the water and whizzing it into a froth. Which she calmly arranged on Max's upper lip and chin.

'Hey!' yelled Max, whisking it off and transferring it

to her face instead. 'It's not working,' he whispered under his breath. 'I'll soap him down, you carry on being daft and then we'll ignore him and have some fun as if he's not there. He'll enjoy himself, I'm sure.'

So Laura settled down to some serious floating and sinking. She snatched Perran's wet flannel from Max and dropped it onto a bowl. 'Wheeee!' she cried, clapping with satisfaction when everyone was duly splattered with water.

Max jumped to his feet. 'Never knew bathtime could be so much fun,' he said in an aside, and then, 'Keeeeowwww!' he yelled, dive-bombing Laura's favourite saucepan lid.

'You devil!' She laughed, her eyes dancing in delight. 'You can have a foam hat for doing that—'

'Help!' protested Max, moving only a feeble inch away so that she could succeed. 'Perran! Help me!'

Laura gave her nephew a quick look. The little mouth was pinched in, the huge eyes close to tears. The grin faded from her face.

'Sweetheart—' she began gently.

Perran grabbed a saucepan lid filled with water and flung it at Max, who unexpectedly dissolved in laughter, rolling on the floor in hysterics.

Laura and Perran exchanged wide-eyed, open-mouthed glances. Then she giggled. But the little boy had turned his back and was pulling out the plug.

'You win,' Max said to him cheerfully, covering him entirely in a large bath towel and hauling him out. 'Wait a minute! Laura, where's Perran? I had him a moment ago...'

There was a flurry of fists from inside the towel, and then a small, flushed face emerged.

'There you are!' Max pretended not to notice Perran's scowl. 'Has Aunty Laura seen your pyjamas?' he asked, busy drying ten protesting toes.

Amazed at Max's good-naturedness—and his paternal skills—Laura picked up the blue striped top with two sleepy hedgehogs wearing nightcaps on the front. 'I wish I had a pair like this,' she enthused, turning them over. 'Oh, Max!' she cried. 'Look, this shows their back view!' She flicked the bobbles on the nightcaps, her face wistful. She could feel tenderness oozing out of her and longed to kiss Perran's rosy cheeks.

Afraid of her feelings, she knew she would be caught up in an emotional turmoil if she prolonged these moments of family togetherness.

'Time's getting on, and you've had a long day, Max,' she said briskly. 'I'll clear up in here, then see what I can do for supper while you settle Perran. OK?'

'My pleasure.'

Max was engrossed in dressing Perran, his lashes long and black on his cheeks, like his son's. Hastily she kissed Perran goodnight. 'Sleep tight,' she said fondly, watching the two of them disappear.

She tidied up as quietly as she could because she wanted to listen in case her nephew said anything. All she could hear, however, was Max telling the story of *The Three Billy Goats Gruff* with such enthusiastic dramatisations of trolls going thumpety-thump over the little wooden bridge that tears welled up in her eyes, and she hurried downstairs to the kitchen to escape. Unnerved by Max's potential brilliance as a father, she did her own thumpety-thumping around and slammed a few pots about.

Then she stubbed her toe on a huge box, half protruding from beneath the kitchen table. Muttering in annoyance, she peeked inside. 'Well, I'll be damned!' she cried, lifting out a tin of artichoke hearts. She dived in to see what other goodies lay in wait. 'Asparagus? Lobster bisque?'

Laura unpacked. Gourmet groceries! Increasingly

Play TIC-TAC-TOE and get FREE GIFTS!

HOW TO PLAY:

1. Play the tic-tac-toe scratch-off game at the right for your FREE BOOKS and FREE GIFT!

2. Send back this card and you'll receive TWO brand-new Harlequin Presents® novels. These books have a cover price of $3.75 each, but they are yours to keep absolutely free.

3. There's no catch. You're under no obligation to buy anything. We charge nothing — ZERO — for your first shipment. And you don't have to make any minimum number of purchases — not even one!

4. The fact is, thousands of readers enjoy receiving books by mail from the Harlequin Reader Service® months before they're available in stores. They like the convenience of home delivery, and they love our discount prices!

5. We hope that after receiving your free books you'll want to remain a subscriber. But the choice is yours — to continue or cancel, any time at all! So why not take us up on our invitation, with no risk of any kind. You'll be glad you did!

YOURS **FREE**
A FABULOUS MYSTERY GIFT!

**We can't tell you what it is…
but we're sure you'll like it!**

A FREE GIFT –
just for playing
TIC-TAC-TOE!

First, scratch the gold boxes on the tic-tac-toe board. Then remove the "X" sticker from the front and affix it so that you get three X's in a row. This means you can get TWO FREE Harlequin Presents® novels and a **FREE MYSTERY GIFT!**

PLAY TIC-TAC-TOE

YES! Please send me all the gifts for which I qualify. I understand that I am under no obligation to purchase any books, as explained on the back of this card.

(U-H-P-08/98)

106 HDL CH5Z

Name

(PLEASE PRINT CLEARLY)

Address _____ Apt.#

City _____ State _____ Zip

The Harlequin Reader Service® — Here's how it works:

Accepting free books places you under no obligation to buy anything. You may keep the books and gift and return the shipping statement marked "cancel." If you do not cancel, about a month later we'll send you 6 additional novels and bill you just $3.12 each, plus 25¢ delivery per book and applicable sales tax, if any.* That's the complete price — and compared to cover prices of $3.75 each — quite a bargain! You may cancel at any time, but if you choose to continue, every month we'll send you 6 more books, which you may either purchase at the discount price...or return to us and cancel your subscription.

*Terms and prices subject to change without notice. Sales tax applicable in N.Y.

amazed, she brought out fine wines, gin, whisky and brandy, chilled smoked salmon, chanterelles, king prawns, organic chicken and an assortment of prime quality vegetables and wildly expensive fruits. All from Harrods. Supper was going to be somewhat of a feast!

She gathered the ingredients she wanted for a simple pasta dish, wondering if the food had been bought for her...or for both of them. Had Max known they would be together? She was worryingly unsure of his motives, his intentions—and her own heart.

Was she glad because he was here? Or would she be relieved to get home? She heard Max coming down the stairs and arranged her features in an expression of neutrality.

'Peace at last!' he announced as he entered, throwing himself into the kitchen's only easy chair. It creaked ominously but he ignored it.

'That's what you think.'

'Oh, God!' he groaned. 'You're not declaring war, are you?'

Laura was surprising herself. She was managing to find the preparation of the pasta sauce of more interest than Max's second change of clean clothes that evening—even though the suede jeans shrieked to be stroked again and the soft cream cashmere sweater contrasted wonderfully with his dark good looks.

'No. But I'm not cooking supper on my own.' She pushed a hand through her hair to see if it was dry. Almost—but it had decided to curl in as many directions as possible. She sighed, giving up on it. 'Find a pinny and chop these onions, will you?'

'I'll cry.'

'Most probably.' Maliciously, she'd kept them specially for him.

Max sighed and unwound his rangy body. Tucking a teatowel into his belt and picking up an onion, he mused,

'Perran wasn't exactly vociferous, was he? We made all the noise.'

Laura allowed herself a little smile. 'We can't do much more,' she said, rapidly deseeding tomatoes, 'other than show him we're to be trusted.' She put her knife down, her face troubled. 'You do think he's all right, don't you?'

'Sure.' Max hacked at the onion inexpertly.

She watched him from under her lashes. He seemed bemused and uncertain, as if he hadn't any idea what he was doing. Touched by his helplessness, she took the knife and showed him what to do.

'I should have brought *Cookery for Beginners* to match your *Bringing Up Baby* book,' she remarked drily.

He didn't bat an eyelid, but continued to frown in concentration, trying to replicate her perfectly diced onion-half. He'd never looked more desirable.

'That was my secretary's brainwave.' He'd done the horizontal slices and was going for the vertical, his attention—apparently—totally focused on the task in hand. 'When she met me at the airport, I discovered that she'd placed it on top of the box of groceries I'd asked her to provide for you.'

She thought that was a little unlikely. 'My, what a gem,' she said sardonically, noticing that Max had succeeded beyond his own wildest dreams and her expectations and was beaming at his neatly diced onion in a touching delight to equal Perran's. Without comment, Laura swept the onion bits into the saucepan and started frying.

'She's funny and thoughtful, madly efficient, and bullies me like hell,' he said fondly.

For some reason, Laura didn't want to hear about this paragon. 'You'd got everything ready for me, hadn't you? Baby book, nappies, baby toiletries, food... What if I'd told you to go ahead and put the children into care?'

'I would have given the baby stuff to the Social Services, taken the food home for a pig-out and kept the book for future reference. Incidentally,' he said casually, pushing his mobile at her, 'do you want to phone Luke?'

'What for?'

'Because he'll have heard the gale reports and will be wondering if you arrived safely. Or... would his wife answer? Would that be a problem...?'

'Max,' she said wearily, 'Luke is happily married. He's my boss and that's all. If you really want to know why he was hugging me, it was because I'd been ratty that morning and I'd told him an ex-lover of mine was turning up... and that he'd been curt and bullying on the phone,' she hurried on, 'and I thought he intended to give me some grief.'

For several heart-stopping seconds he stared at her tense face.

'It's the truth!' she yelled, unable to bear his appraisal.

'So you don't want to ring him?'

'No!'

'So,' persisted Max cheerfully, pushing her to screaming point, 'when you were upset about leaving—'

'Oh, give it a rest, will you?' she jerked out, bashing the onions so vigorously with the wooden spoon that they almost left the pan entirely. 'I—I was upset about the children. And Fay and Daniel.'

'Y-e-s.' He didn't sound very convinced.

'Don't hassle me,' she complained.

Infuriatingly, he ruffled her hair. Laura exaggeratedly slammed her hand on her head to smooth it down again. Max laughed and caught her hand in his.

'You're leaving bits of onion in it,' he said gently. 'Stand still, I'll get them out.'

Laura stopped breathing. He was taking an awful long

time finding a few scraps of onion, and she was enjoying the experience far too much for it to be good for her. She sought frantically for something to slice through the growing feeling that Max's hands, now on her shoulders, would slide to her waist and...

'Monkeys in a zoo!' she blurted out.

His lazily smiling eyes met hers. 'What is?'

She wanted to crawl under the floorboards. Only tongue-tied teenagers could have made their feelings more obvious. 'You, picking bits out of my hair. Like fleas,' she floundered, wishing she'd never started.

He produced his rich, low chuckle, targeting her fragile nerves and hitting them bang on. 'You're priceless, Laura,' he murmured fondly. 'I've always loved your sense of humour. I've never laughed as much as the times we—'

'Is it all gone?' she cried in panic.

He sighed. 'I'm tired. I'm a bit slow on the uptake so you'll have to explain the cryptics. Is what gone?'

'The onion.'

'Yes!' he said, laughing again. Laura felt stupid. He ruffled her hair again and she jumped back.

'Sorry. It's so touchable.'

'I hate you doing that,' she lied, still zinging from the incidental massage from his strong, sensitive fingers. 'It makes me feel like...like...'

'A dog, a monkey or an elephant?'

Her mouth quirked, then she got control over it. 'A dim-witted pet being patronised by its master. So keep your hands off or I might bite.'

'I'll do my best. Shall I check on Kerenza again?' he asked helpfully. 'Or would you prefer to go?'

With bent head, her hair swinging forward to mask her instant paleness, she said curtly, 'I'm cooking. You do it.'

'Delighted. Shan't be long.'

'Take all the time you like,' she told him sourly.

Hearing him tiptoeing up the stairs, Laura reflected that he'd been in and out of the children's bedroom like a yo-yo. She hadn't set foot in it yet.

'They're both OK.' A breathless, shining-eyed Max bounded back into the kitchen. 'Perran's sleeping with his bottom in the air and his head to one side so his mouth's scrunched up. He's got eyelashes that could bat for England, hasn't he? And I had to stroke Kerenza's hair; it's so silky and fine. Doesn't she sleep a lot?'

He's enjoying this, she thought bleakly, hurling the fresh tagliatelle into the saucepan. 'Five minutes.'

Close to flinging the whole contents of the pan over him, Laura smacked the wooden spoon into the middle of the onions and gave them a beating instead.

He came to inspect progress, fetching up a hair's breadth from her rigid back. 'Five minutes! That was quick! Cooking's a doddle, really, isn't it?' He grinned when she threw him a 'little do you know' scowl over her shoulder. 'OK. I concede that chops or boeuf en croute might be more of a challenge...'

'Why don't you open the wine?' she suggested tightly.

He was too close. She needed space to breathe, privacy to let her face crumple... Oh, God! she needed release from this eternal wrenching and twisting of all her emotions! She felt ragged inside, sore and torn, as if the gale had set up its own storm inside her mind, heart and body.

'Good idea.'

He drifted off. His chirpiness was going to drive her mad, she thought, dipping her fingers into the boiling water without caring that it hurt, and testing the pasta. And all the while he was humming 'Life Is Just A Bowl Of Cherries'.

She'd kill him before the evening was out. She drained the pasta noisily. Either that, or she'd slam him against a wall and kiss that damn smile right off his cheerful face…

A shocking spurt of fire seared from her loins to her breast and she nearly dropped the colander. Shocked at her own thoughts, she banged it down on the formica top and clattered about, clearing up some of the cooking utensils.

'Getting quite cosy, isn't it? Us tucked up like an old married couple in the warm, supper on the go, the gale out there,' Max said with a stupefying satisfaction and an expression of smug bliss.

'Lay up!'

'I've often wondered,' he said, quite unperturbed by her snarling order, 'what I'd be like as a father.' Absently he selected cutlery. 'I think I might be rather good.'

Often wondered? How cruel could life be? She gripped the handle of the empty pasta saucepan, not noticing how hot it was. You fool! she wanted to yell. You are a father! Can't you recognise your own son?

Why hadn't he wanted to be a father five years ago? Why hadn't he wanted a family as much as he clearly did now? And why did he have to keep shoving his happy daddy act in her face all the time?

It really hurt. She felt excluded from an exclusive club she wanted to join. She wanted a baby. Someone to call her Mother.

Dammit! Why was she torturing herself? Maybe, if he knew what had happened to her, he'd choose his words more carefully and stop breaking her heart. But she couldn't bring herself to tell him. She'd howl for days. And what use would that be to Perran and Kerenza?

Grimly she crushed an excessive amount of garlic into the onion pan and contemplated adding a bucket of chillies. And forcibly stuffing the mixture down his throat with the entire frying pan itself to follow.

'Fabulous aroma,' he murmured, appearing at her side. 'I'm passionate about garlic. Here's your wine. Cheers.'

She lifted a flushed, vile-tempered face. 'What could we possibly be cheering about?' she muttered, taking a huge gulp.

'Our good fortune!'

Laura pushed irascibly at the lock of damp hair which his outrush of breath had dislodged. '*This* is good fortune?' she scathed, angrily shovelling the fresh tomato sauce and king prawns into the pan. 'A miserable little cottage, a ferocious gale and stair-rods of rain outside, two strange children and—and...' Her voice wobbled, betraying her pent-up emotions. 'And...worst of all *you*!'

'Laura,' he said gently.

'Shut up while I'm assembling, will you?' she flared.

She wanted a row. Hostility. Anything but gentleness and that evilly warm, rich voice, slipping effortlessly into her body and threatening to loosen her inhibitions so that she flung her arms around his neck and clung there, indulging herself in his intensely male comfort.

He shut up. But only until they were sitting at the table—she on the edge of her chair and as taut as a wire, he relaxed, concerned, friendly...everything she didn't want him to be. Including handsome and sexy and the kind of man she'd love to see across the table every day of her life.

Was she stupid or what?

They ate in a tense silence. He kept looking at her, and she stared fixedly at her plate but nevertheless felt the vibrations between them with every inch of her body. Her hand shook when she sipped her wine and it spilled on the table.

When he dabbed at it with his handkerchief, he obviously caught a glimpse of the tell-tale teardrop which had trickled down the side of her nose, because he tipped up her chin and scooped up the tear with his forefinger.

'It's me, isn't it?' he murmured.

'Yes, it's you!' Almost hysterical, she plunged her fork into a defenceless prawn and the tines screeched in protest against the china plate, setting her teeth on edge. 'This is me and that is you! Is this an identity crisis? Who the devil else do you think you are?'

'Oh, come *on*, Laura! You know what I meant. You're finding it tough being with me because we were lovers. But that was a long time ago. We're over any embarrassment, aren't we?'

It was on the tip of her tongue to say, You are, because it was meaningless. I'm not. I have too many scars.

Unable to face him with the truth, she chewed the suddenly tasteless prawn and looked for something else on her plate to attack. It was that, or go down for murder. Spearing every mushroom she could find, she finally decided to say with ridiculously prim hauteur, 'Over, but not forgotten.'

'Look at me,' he said quietly.

'No, thanks.'

'Scared?' he taunted.

'Disobedient.'

He threw his head back and laughed in delight, prompting her to look up. 'Disobedient, eh?' he whispered softly.

Her huge, pained eyes locked with his.

It was, she thought hazily, one of those extraordinary moments when everything seems to stop, when you read someone's soul like a book and you know, know for absolute certain, that this is the person who is right for you...with no logical reason for knowing that...and a million reasons why you should be wrong...only, despite everything, you feel a quiet conviction so deep that it can only be true.

She and Max were made for one another, their minds and souls linked like two halves of a coin...completing one another...complementing one another, destined to be together.

Man and woman, Adam and Eve, Max and Laura.

He felt the same—she knew that too, with a confidence and a thrill of excitement that clutched at her tender heart and sent her pulses haywire.

The moment stretched into minutes. She and Max remained utterly transfixed. Suddenly solemn, they held their breath in case the slightest movement should break the spell and spin them back into reality.

Holding her gaze, he slowly stood up and walked around the table. She didn't want to move away. If she'd had any sense she would have made some light quip and avoided the inevitable, but she sat there, waiting, anticipating, the tension rising in her body till she could barely contain it.

Worse...she blatantly encouraged him, lifting her radiantly hopeful face to his. He was going to kiss her and she had no intention of stopping him.

'Don't stand up,' he breathed.

She stood up.

Max dragged in a strangled breath. His eyes were black and smouldering and his breath came hot and heavy on her burning forehead, but she was barely breathing at all.

'Laura...' He spoke her name with infinite tenderness, caressing it so sensually that she quivered as though naked before him. He didn't touch her, but she was aware that every inch of him strained to do so. Huskily, shakily, he said, 'Don't let me kiss you.'

Joyfully disobedient, and trembling from helpless adoration, she lifted up her arms. Then he pulled her to his body with a low cry, spanning her waist, moving his hands up her small, exquisite back as if he'd long starved for the touch of her.

The spell was broken and all was whirling, intoxicating sensation. Laura groaned as he pressed her hard against him, pushing her breasts into his chest so that she—and he—felt the hard thrust of each aroused peak. His hands tugged at her shirt and she gasped, her lips searching for his in a desperate bid for satisfaction.

This was where she ought to be, where she'd wanted to be all those long, lonely years. The warmth, the smell, the feel of him... Firm, enclosing, secure...

I love him. I'd barter anything to be with him, to be loved in return. *Love me!* She gave a low moan. Oh, God! She wanted him! And he looked back at her helplessly, as though he hardly dared to trust what was happening.

It was she who finally cracked, pulling his dark head down to hers, covering his arching mouth in a fierce and passionate kiss that went on and on till she felt faint and breathless, her head spinning with delirium.

One of his hands crept tantalisingly up her spine, caressing her skin as if it were silk, loving each vertebra in a slow, tortuous and painfully erotic slide which left her weakly anticipating his next move. His other hand slipped between their bodies and found her breast. Laura's head swam in a mist of sensation till suddenly she was compelled to feel his skin against hers and her fingers were frantically pulling at his sweater and she was moaning under her breath in frustration at the barrier between them.

For a brief moment he broke free, the cashmere was shrugged over his head and he was with her again, his mouth warm and moist on hers while she feverishly attacked his shirt buttons and...finally...touched him.

She felt the tremor rippling beneath his taut skin and

was glad she could do this to him. Her head went back in silent exultation as the rest of her body stilled so that she could revel in the feel of him beneath her tentatively exploring fingers.

'You're as smooth as satin,' she whispered, pressing her mouth to his ribs.

'God! Laura!' he muttered harshly, dragging her up, his mouth savaging her throat. 'You're beautiful,' he mumbled. 'More lovely than I ever remember. I wanted you the moment I set eyes on you...always have... always will...'

She staggered a little, dazed by what he was saying, hardly daring to believe it. But his whole body shook with suppressed passion, each muscle painfully taut and quivering as her hands touched, stroked, loved, moved on.

She was close to tears with joy and unable to think of anything but that he wanted her as much as she wanted him.

Her body ached to sink into his, to melt in the heat they were generating till there was no space, no separateness between them at all.

In response to her frenzied pressure he shifted his hips, and a shudder ran through her whole fragile length. The sexual excitement between them was unbelievable. It consumed her utterly, and she just wanted to grab and snatch and devour him, she felt so hungry. And her passion was intensified by the knowledge that Max's self-control hung on a slender thread.

Suddenly leaving her, he grabbed the plates and flung them anyhow onto the draining board. It was a wonderfully uncharacteristic action on his part, and it thrilled her.

She felt her supple body being bent back over the table. Max's weight descended, his mouth searching hers, his tongue delving deep while he began to strip her with a clumsy, frantic haste which was so endearing to her that she could hardly bear it.

Her eyes closed in longing. Cool air drifted over her breasts and they swelled, their tips hardening in an instant as they waited eagerly for his touch.

His lips wandered hotly to the hollow of her throat and then his tongue slicked along her collar-bone. Laura's fingers tightened convulsively in his silky hair. She was unable to wait, needing something to break the tension.

'Kiss me *hard*!' she begged in agony.

'My darling Laura…' His mouth covered hers. They were both shaking. She arched her body, inviting him like an experienced wanton.

His breath rasped out in an anguished groan and then his palms were moving gently over each painful nipple, making Laura jerk with pleasure and totally lose all her inhibitions. Her legs wrapped around his hips. She drew him down to her, and he slid her further along the table, his drugged, feral eyes now burning into hers.

'Touch me…everywhere…' she whispered in a dry croak, mesmerised by him, by her overpowering desires, by the overwhelming emotions clamouring in her brain.

His eyes glittered. His hands closed on the waistband of her jeans, and she shook with shock at the stabs of crippling need which burned and liquidised her body and set it on fire.

Her eyes pleaded with his. Gently she touched his face and he bent to kiss her, so sweetly that her limbs melded with his and she felt so deliriously happy that she wanted to cry.

She loved this man dearly. And would do so for ever. The pain and delight mingled together in a heartbreaking bitter-sweetness.

'Laura,' he said tenderly into her softly crushed mouth.

She sighed into his ear while he kissed her with a thoroughness that sent her heart thudding violently against his chest.

'I want you!' he whispered. 'No...I want more than that.' He stared deeply into her eyes. 'You know how I feel.'

She nodded.

Max hesitated. Then said very quietly, 'I want to love you, Laura.'

'Then love me,' she breathed, all tension vanishing with those words.

'I must take care of you. But I don't have... Oh, hell, Laura!' he cried in wretched agony.

She frowned, confused, then realised what he meant. Tears stung her eyes. He didn't have to take precautions. It didn't matter. She gave a piteous cry, and suddenly Max was stroking her hair, kissing her face gently.

'What is it, Laura?' he asked, licking up the salty tears.

'I—I can't...' She looked at his anxious, caring face and buried her head in his shoulder. 'It's all right. I'm OK. It doesn't matter. I want you,' she said brokenly. 'But...'

'Not on a wooden table?'

She smiled reluctantly through a veil of tears. 'I don't care,' she answered honestly. 'Anywhere...' She gulped at the flash of dark desire in his eyes. And reached out for what she wanted. Max. 'Yes.' Her fingers stroked his beautiful, pained face. 'It's all right,' she promised. 'I'm safe.'

'You said...anywhere...' he whispered into her mouth, her shoulder, her lifting breast. 'Here...and here...'

Laura closed her eyes and gave herself to unthinking pleasure. Her hands trailed through his hair and she pressed her lips to his forehead. She loved him. This must be right. They were so perfectly matched. Exquisite torture...

'Yes...!' She gasped as his lips enclosed a nipple and a great, hot wave of desire engulfed her. And she knew that Max couldn't stop now, that he felt the same renewed excitement she did, the fast beat of their pulses firing their bodies, urging them on to writhe and torment, to suckle and nibble, murmur, sigh, gasp hoarsely...

Flesh to flesh. Naked. The slide of his body, the concentration as they fused and clung, questing with their hands, driven by madness for the total release of intolerable strains on their perspiring, tangling bodies.

'Oh, Laura!' His voice...breaking, desperate. He pulled her up and slid her gently onto him.

'Max...!' Just a whisper. It was all she could manage because she was dying in the delight of his silky smoothness, the feel of her own liquid heat surrounding him, easing their slow, sensual movements.

He kissed her very tenderly, very lovingly, his fingers stimulating her breasts, massaging, circling, flicking... Her hands went to his shoulders, her eyes adored him, and she shook beneath him till she groaned aloud.

'Max! Please...!'

He moved as she'd wanted him to move. Gathering strength, faster, faster, kissing her all the while, muttering foolish things into her mouth about loving her, worshipping her, needing her, fanning her excitement till she felt a savagery inhabit her body and she thrashed and bucked and twisted sinuously to deepen the sensations exploding in every vein and pore, in her very brain.

Max was groaning, but she could only hear him dimly as orgasm after orgasm ripped through her, tearing the life from her sensitised body till they both sank in an exhausted stupor, hot, panting and sated, drawn close in each other's arms.

'I can't believe it,' he whispered. 'Never knew I could feel like this...'

She couldn't speak, but allowed a feeble, 'Mmm,' of agreement to drift from her softly parted lips.

He shifted his weight and held her tightly. Neither of them spoke. A happy warmth stole over Laura. She felt herself melting into him, into the table, towards somewhere dreamy and velvety-dark. And she let herself go, not caring about the future, the past, the present.

Some time through her passion-drugged sleep she was aware that Max was carrying her upstairs. Then she felt the softness of a bed, a puff of air as a duvet covered her. She curled up like a child, and Max's body, warm and welcome, snuggled into her back.

Too sleepy to indicate her awareness with even a sigh of pleasure, she smiled to herself when he positioned himself so that his chest lay against her spine, his pelvis curved around her soft, rounded rear and his legs folded themselves to hers.

He wanted the maximum amount of skin to touch her, she thought happily, accepting the butterfly kisses on her shoulder and earlobe with contentment.

She lay there in a state of bliss. She had no reason to feel sure of him, but she did, and that gave her a warm, drowsy serenity through the whole of her body as she felt him relax and begin to breathe more deeply.

Their love-making hadn't been like that the first time. It had happened quickly—with the same passion and urgency, yes—but with desperation, because Max had been leaving for Paris and neither of them had paid any special attention to arousing one another.

We were greedy, she thought, more awake now, listening to the howling gale and the rain battering the window. Selfish. Why should it be so different this time? Her mind still felt dazed by the depth of her feelings and the intensity of their love-making.

She shivered suddenly. Only one of them could have had any practice since then. He'd made love to Fay. How many more women?

From outside, above the noise of the wind and rain, came a sound that chilled her even more. A maroon. The lifeboat was on call.

Laura froze. She felt compelled to slide out of bed even though she knew she'd see nothing. Hastily pulling her shirt and jeans over her naked body, she padded to the window. Nothing. Pitch-darkness.

Her nose pressed to the cold glass as she relived the terrible night her father had gone out to his death. 'God help those poor souls,' she whispered fervently.

She turned and looked at the sleeping Max. A pang of love stirred her body as she stared at his slumbering, blissful face. Life was so uncertain. You couldn't waste a moment. But...

Her emotions were confused, her nerves ragged. However much she loved him, she couldn't pretend that there would be a future for them. Even if he wasn't fickle and untrustworthy, he wanted children; she was barren.

She heaved a pained sigh, unable, unwilling to imagine what would happen to them both. But she thought of the things her mother had said the day of her father's funeral. Every sentence had begun with 'I wish' or 'If only'.

Laura knew she had the chance of happiness, however brief. And she'd take that, however long or short it might turn out to be. No strings. She and Max... Together for a few days, a week, a month... It would be worth it, even the pain of the inevitable goodbye. OK, she'd be hurt. But so be it.

Suddenly restless, scared of her decision, she wandered out to the landing, intending to make a warm drink. Or... She paused by the door of the small bedroom. She could get over the hurdle of seeing Kerenza without Max around.

For a few moments she dithered. Then, with her heart in her mouth, she tiptoed into the small bedroom and knelt by the carry-cot on the floor.

Kerenza's tiny beauty stabbed at her heart. She looked so vulnerable and helpless. Laura ached to know what it would be like to hold your living, newborn baby in your arms, to touch its tiny fingers and ears and to marvel that a moment of love could create something so perfect and beautiful.

Tentatively she reached out a shaking hand and touched the pretty blonde curls. Her instincts were to snatch the baby up and hold her tightly. Instead, she withdrew her hand and shut her eyes, seeing herself cradling Kerenza in her arms, walking up and down the room, singing her to sleep. Loving her.

She drew in a jagged gulp of air. Never her own baby. She'd blown her chance for that. This would be the closest she ever came to knowing how a mother felt.

She wanted Max for all his faults, driven by something even stronger than her knowledge of his weakness and infidelities. And she wanted his children, with a desperation that tore her in two.

The tears streamed silently down her face because of the hopelessness of her dearest desire. Wretchedly she picked up a soft teddy bear and clutched it to her tightly, rocking backwards and forwards, weeping with the emptiness in her heart, the hollowness of her ruined body.

Kerenza began to cry too. Through the sheeting curtains of her own tears, Laura stared, incapable of doing anything, shaking like a leaf from the shattering release of her deepest emotions. Numb, appalled at the thought that she would have to pick up the baby, soothe her, act like a real mother...she choked on a shuddering sob.

And gazed at the distressed baby with huge, flooding blue eyes, willing herself to make that fatal move.

'Laura, sweetheart!'

'Oh, no!'

She crumpled to the floor, mortified by Max's appearance and the sound of his low, tender voice.

'Hang on in there,' he said.

Her hands covered her head as if to hide her grief as he came past her, and she heard Kerenza's cry suddenly cut off.

Max could be heard walking about with Kerenza, kissing her, murmuring to her. 'So, poppet, we'll put you down here...and take off that nasty wet nappy... That's better. Give me a smile—gorgeous! Um...wipes...there. Don't you waggle your little legs about! I'm new at this game! Nappy...this way round—no, this. Oh, hell! Right the first time. Tear off the side strips, press, stick, bingo! All right, little lovely?' Kerenza started grizzling. 'Ah. I feared as much. Laura...'

She stayed locked in her misery, screwed even tighter into a desolate heap, like someone shielding themselves from an explosion.

'I need you,' he said gently. 'One of us has to hold Kerenza, the other has to make up the feed. I've no idea how women do this on their own, but I certainly can't. Please, Laura. I need help.'

Without a word she stumbled to her feet, rubbed her eyes and went down to the kitchen. Followed by Max. Wearing only a cream towelling robe, he walked up and down, joggling Kerenza, sitting her on his shoulder, flying her around the room.

Breaking Laura's heart.

With the aid of Fay's scrawled instructions by the sterilising unit, she somehow made up the formula and passed the bottle to Max, carefully avoiding his eyes.

'You feed her,' he said generously. 'I'm sure you'd love to.'

She flinched, hung her head and hugged her freezing body. 'No!'

'Then you will sit here while I feed the baby and you'll tell me what's upset you.'

The baby lay contentedly in Max's arms, suckling at the bottle. Laura risked a look at him and her heart turned over. There was an expression of wonderful tenderness on his face that she'd never seen before. Awe, love and protectiveness all rolled into one. The kind of look worn by new fathers the world over—and which tugged devastatingly at the heartstrings of any onlooker.

She hadn't realised she'd be so affected by the sight of Max with the baby. Perran, yes—and she still had that to cope with. But this... She sat down hurriedly and stared blindly at the tabletop. Then remembered what had recently happened there, and blushed furiously.

'Come here, darling,' Max crooned.

She bit her lip, paralysed at the thought of being so close to the baby. Max made that decision for her. He moved his chair so his body was pressed close to hers, and for a while there was silence, broken only by Kerenza greedily taking her feed.

'Put your head on my shoulder and tell me everything,' he urged softly. 'We can't have secrets, can we?'

She wasn't ready. Couldn't bring herself to say what had happened. But he was waiting for an explanation. 'I—I woke up...'

'Yes,' he encouraged.

And then she found her reason for crying—one Max would accept. One which would leave her secrets where they belonged, hidden from sight in her mind.

'The maroon went off. The lifeboat's out there, Max.'

And she didn't know if she snuggled against him for sympathy or because she had to hide her guilty face. She hated herself for using that as an excuse. But it had started her emotions on their downhill run and put her in a mood of depression.

He leaned sideways and kissed her pale, ice-cold cheek. 'I understand. It must be hard for you, a night like this. They're brave men, every one of them. I don't envy what they have to do. God bring them back safely, and whoever's out there in trouble.' He gave her a hug. 'Go back to bed, darling. I'll put Kerenza down. She's asleep—look.'

Laura stole a glance. Kerenza had fallen into a deep sleep in mid-suck. The little face was sweetly crumpled, fair lashes glinting, the mouth stuck in a pursed-up shape around the teat. Laura smiled wistfully.

'Adorable.' Without thinking, she said, 'I don't know how Fay could call her a mis—' Horrified, she pressed her lips together.

'A mistake?' suggested Max shrewdly. His face darkened. 'Your sister doesn't deserve kids like these!'

'I'm sure it was one of those things mothers say in jest,' Laura defended.

'Hmm. Well, take Kerenza while I wash out the bottle, would you?' he asked casually.

'No!' she whispered, drawing back.

Without comment, Max stood up and tucked the sleeping baby safely into the corner of the armchair. When he began to rinse the bottle, Laura fled up the stairs and dived under the duvet, burying her face in the pillow.

She heard Max come in and shed his robe. The bed depressed and then he was turning her around. Her pulses raced. She knew he was going to demand to know why she wouldn't touch Kerenza.

CHAPTER SIX

THE door banged against the wall. They both leapt apart guiltily.

'What the...? Perran! What's the matter?' asked Max, recovering himself first.

The little boy stood quivering in the doorway, as if petrified. Laura slid out of bed and ran over, crouching down beside him.

'Was it the storm, darling?' she asked sympathetically.

Perran's mouth wobbled out of control. He flung himself onto the bed and scrabbled to the top, burrowing down next to Max, who bent his head and murmured something soothing. Laura felt her heart lurch. Two dark heads. Father and son.

'Come on, Laura,' said Max. 'There's room for you too. Let's get some sleep.'

She made a face, hearing the first whimpers from the small bedroom. 'I don't think we're in luck. The baby's awake.'

'Bring her in,' suggested Max, occupied with soothing Perran. 'Perhaps I didn't burp her properly.'

'I—' She hesitated, and Max raised an eyebrow in query. 'All right,' she muttered, seeing she couldn't refuse.

Quickly she marched into the other room, picked up the grizzling child and returned, walking up and down, rubbing Kerenza's little back and thinking of elephants and monkeys and dogs. Anything but babies and how sweet they smelled, how soft they were...

Kerenza startled them all with a huge burp and they laughed. Even Perran. But she kept on grizzling.

'Laura.' Max had turned back the duvet. 'You'll freeze. Bring her in and let's make it a foursome. It's getting light outside already. We might manage an hour or two's sleep before they're demanding breakfast again.'

'Good idea,' she said, bone-weary.

He sighed contentedly, reached out an arm and stroked Kerenza's blonde head till she fell asleep. Then the back of his hand brushed Laura's drowsy face.

'Like happy families. Sleep well,' he said softly.

She kept her hands stiffly by her sides for a long time, determined not to love them all. And failed miserably. Max had dropped off to sleep already, his profile dark and beautiful against the white of the pillow. Perran had snuggled into the circle of his father's arm, a worshipper already. Kerenza...

Laura's finger hesitantly stretched out. She traced the button nose, the squidgy little lips, the putty chin. And kissed the baby's cheek...and lost her heart entirely.

So much for her resolutions. All broken. What a weakling she was!

'No, Perran, not on the table, get off, there's a good boy—and get your foot out of the sugar bowl... Oh, Perran!' she cried in exasperation, jiggling the baby in one arm and stirring home-made soup with the other. How did parents manage? Two days in the cottage with rain pelting down in sheer, unbroken sheets, and she was going crazy!

'Hi! I'm home!'

Both she and Perran raced to meet Max. Fred screeched as he always did when he heard Max's voice. Perran crashed violently into Max's shins and wrapped his arms around them like octopus tentacles; Laura skidded to a stop and leaned forward for her kiss.

'Wonderful to see you!' she said, passing him Kerenza.

'Oh, golly gosh!' he simpered coyly.

'Nothing to do with your dazzling charm,' Laura informed him, the glow in her eyes giving the lie to that. 'You're wanted on the baby-minding front. You should *see* the kitchen!' she said, chattering on as she made her way back, with Max shuffling along, hampered by Perran's weight. 'We've been making rolls for lunch.'

'I'd never have guessed,' he lied outrageously, kissing her flour-enhanced eyebrows and reeling at the choking white flour dust everywhere. 'Smells delicious. How clever of you, Perran! Er...where are these rolls?'

Releasing his hold, his son dashed for the bread basket, managing to overturn a chair and almost knock a bowl off the table as he did so.

'I can see where he gets his boisterous nature from,' mused Max, putting Kerenza into her chair.

Laura paused, the soup ladle in her hand, then plunged it into the big saucepan. 'Oh?' she squeaked.

'He's so like you,' said Max affectionately.

'Me?' Laura almost threw the ladleful of soup onto the lino in surprise.

'Eager. Enthusiastic. Rather like your father, too. Same dark hair, strong, Celtic colouring. Oh, fabulous, Perran!' he said, when presented with the basket, unaware that Laura was frozen, stunned by Max's deduction. 'Which is mine? Can I eat it now?' The roll was crammed clumsily into his hand. Max put it on his plate, and patted the chair next to him. 'Come and sit down. No. Second thoughts, go and charm Fred into silence, will you? That's terrific. Wow! This is the best roll I've ever tasted! Magic!' he called to Perran's departing back. The little boy turned, beamed proudly and bounced off to see his adored Fred.

'Now,' said Max smugly, 'I've found us the perfect house.'

She jerked into life. 'That's wonderful!' she cried, dealing soup out all round excitedly. 'Soup's ready, Perran!' she called.

The child came clattering back, and she sank into her chair, a warm pink suffusing her skin. With more room, it would be easier to manage...

'And the rain's forecast to stop later today, so we'll be able to get those nannies along for interview,' Max was saying in a sudden rush of words, as if he felt driven to get them off his chest. 'We can return to our previous lives. Can I have another roll, Perran? Or would that be hugely greedy?'

No. No, her brain was screaming. Not so soon. Not when they were all getting on so well... Despite his evident impatience at being cooped up for the past couple of days, Max had been wonderful. A perfect lover, friend, temporary parent.

Strong, sensitive, good-tempered, willing to read the same story over and over again to Perran, to be a horse and gallop up and down the corridor, helping her to teach Perran one or two essential table manners... Making love to her tenderly, fiercely, urgently, lingeringly...

If there had just been the sexual attraction, it would have been easier to walk away from him. She knew he wasn't the kind of guy to value fidelity, and, though the sex was beyond her wildest dreams, she'd rather be without Max than share him.

But everything else was perfect too. Apart from being a wonderful father, she admired him as a man. Listening to the business phone calls he'd made, she'd been impressed by his decisiveness, his easy, relaxed way of doing business, his clearly excellent relationships with other financiers and clients.

And he knew how to make her happy. Insincere or not, he was everything she'd ever wanted in a man.

A little longer with him was all she asked. A little longer with them all.

She knew that Fay and Daniel were likely to remain in custody for the next week; Max's last phone call had established that nothing much would happen and he'd be wasting his time by travelling to Morocco.

Knowing Perran as she now did, and the impact Max had had on the little boy, she realised that he'd be devastated if they left him in the charge of a nanny.

Nor could she bear it.

White-faced, appalled at losing Max so soon, she raised her head, compelled to see whether he felt a twinge of regret at the thought of leaving.

He appeared to be indifferent. 'Shall I...?' His jaw tightened. Perhaps that was why his voice sounded strained. 'Shall I organise that, then?'

She gave a strangled cry and stifled it, clapping her hand over her mouth.

'Problem?' Max asked hoarsely.

'Hot soup!' she invented.

He gave her a cynical stare. 'You've done that once before.' Suddenly free of tension, he leaned back, his eyes narrowed as he assessed the more likely cause of her misery.

To fox him, she swirled her soup around and added salt it didn't need. She didn't trust herself to reply yet. Bubbling up inside her was the longing to fling herself to her knees and beg hysterically for more time with her temporary family. But she must be logical. Persuade Max that the nanny was a bad idea.

Her brow furrowed. Of course, she was playing a dangerous game with her own emotions by staying longer than planned—but this would be her only chance of living her dream.

Every moment had been precious, and she'd devoured each minute with an uninhibited joy, even the endless washing up, the exhaustion, having hardly a moment to herself.

'Coming to a decision, Laura?' Max murmured silkily.

Her head jerked up. He was grinning and indicating her bowl. Laura squirmed with embarrassment as he began to laugh at her. She'd positioned the turnip chunks at twelve o'clock in her bowl, carrots at three o'clock, parsnip at six o'clock, and had been pondering over what to do with the two remaining vegetables.

'Potatoes at nine o'clock, mushrooms in the middle,' Max suggested, almost helpless with laughter.

He didn't care. And was too thick to see that she did! 'It's not funny!' she cried vehemently.

'Yes, it is.'

'I mean about the nanny. I—I'm worried about the children.' She ate twelve o'clock in one mouthful. 'They're being shoved around from pillar to post. Fay leaves, a friend turns up, then leaves, we turn up, then move to a strange house, then leave, a nanny turns up... It's not good for Perran, Max! And he hasn't s-p-o-k-e-n yet,' she said, spelling out the word. 'I think,' she said firmly, thrilled to have found a truly valid reason for delaying the nanny interviews, 'that another change in his routine would ruin everything we've set up.'

'Not necessarily. A nanny would also maintain regular bedtimes, good table manners,' he argued. 'She'd be just as good at enforcing our meals at the table rule—'

'But Max—!' Her heart sank. She gazed at him in dismay, all her lovely plans shattered.

She should have realised. He wanted to go. She and the children meant little to him. He was having fun, yes;

he couldn't fake that. But she couldn't blame him for wanting to leave. He probably missed jetting around the world, wearing business suits and being fawned over by paragon secretaries.

How could elegant dinners in sophisticated restaurants compare with fish and chips or homely stew, with a baby yelling upstairs and Perran's inedible burnt biscuits for pudding?

Her eyes softened. Max had stolidly munched his way through his share. She'd adored him for that.

'You had a "but" hovering somewhere,' he reminded her.

Max's dark head was bent over his soup. She couldn't tell what he was thinking—except when Perran began to dunk his bread too vigorously Max's hand shot out with unusual speed and ruthlessness to stop him. Then, to her surprise, he released his grip, leaned over and kissed his son's chubby cheek in apology.

'Gently,' he said with a smile. 'You'll give the carrots a headache.'

Perran giggled at Max's stupidity and scooped up his soup with the delicacy of a lady at a banquet. Laura smiled sentimentally. He was a very sweet little boy— and she *had* to fight for more time with him. They'd done wonders in a few days. Surely Max must see that?

'I have a big "but",' she said with determination. 'What we're doing is having an effect. There's been a remarkable change in a certain someone's behaviour and you know it. However brilliant a nanny might be, she'll be different. And you-know-who will have to get used to slightly different methods. That's too confusing at this particular moment. You'd be failing as an uncle if you didn't acknowledge that love—family love—is an important ingredient in bringing children up.'

'Y-e-s,' conceded Max.

He was wavering! Delighted, she caught his hand

tightly in hers. 'We can help him, Max! Wouldn't it be wonderful if he really began to trust us and started to communicate? At the moment we still get tantrums and antisocial behaviour. If we could spend—'

'How long?' He stared at her, his eyes as dark as night.

The words 'for ever' almost popped out. She blinked, unable to tear her eyes away. It felt as if she was swimming in the velvety blackness of his gaze, and she had to bite her lip to stop herself asking the impossible. The children belonged to Fay and Daniel and were on loan. As for Max... Well, he belonged to another world, many women.

'I don't know.' *Risk it*, a little voice in her head urged. 'A week?' When Max didn't immediately throw his hands up in horror, she became bolder. 'Perhaps two. With second by second attention we can do a lot in that time and hand over a more normal little boy—maybe even to Fay, if you've been to Marrakesh and managed to get the charge dropped.'

'You're asking a lot there.' Max smoothed her anxious brow with his fingers. 'About Fay and Daniel, I mean, not the two weeks. I agree in principle. However,' he said, smiling at her elated expression, 'you have a job in London to worry about.'

Laura resisted the compulsion to fling her arms around him, but she was buzzing with happiness. 'I'll contact Luke tonight. But I'm sure his sister will be delighted to carry on for a little while longer. Her kiddie's just gone to school, and she's been searching for a job for ages.'

'Two weeks is a long time when you're living every hour together.' He paused. 'It will be hard when we leave,' he added in a low voice.

Brutal. Her stomach muscles clenched in a spasm of misery. In an effort to make the best of the situation, she said, 'We'll keep in touch with the children, won't we? Visit them often, send them postcards—I could write every week and tell them how Fred is, send a little animal card; you know how much Perran loves animals...'

Her voice died to nothing. Max was looking pained. Laura felt his distress keenly. He loved his son. That was obvious from the moment Perran ran into their bedroom in the mornings to when Max watched the sleeping child at night, his face rapt.

By the end of another two weeks he'd love him even more. Maybe he was afraid of the inevitable parting as much as she, and he preferred to cut off the relationship now, before it became unbearably intimate.

Was she asking too much? 'Oh, Max,' she said, a catch in her voice. 'I'm being selfish. I'm putting my point of view and not thinking of you. If it's too difficult—'

'No,' he growled. 'Yes... Oh, hell, Laura, I only know that I'm enjoying myself more than I could ever have imagined. And you're right about Perran needing continuity of care. Yet it'll make it more of a wrench leaving...the children. But, as you say, we can keep in touch.' He smiled fondly at his son. 'Good boy. All finished!' he said approvingly. 'No, leave your spoon in your bowl. It's too mucky to go on the tablecloth.' There was a pause while Max gently wiped Perran's mouth. Then he turned back to Laura. 'I'm not sure,' he said, almost under his breath, 'that I can manage two weeks.'

'Then let's take one day at a time.'

She'd bargain to have an hour, and live that to the full if that was all she could get. Eyes bright with tears, she smiled, trying to cope with the mixture of joy and sadness sweeping through her body.

'Agreed.' Max reached across the table and held her hand in his, squeezing it, making a kind of pact. 'We'll enjoy today and every day we have.'

'I'm glad you've had fun over the last few days,' she said earnestly.

He smiled. 'I've been in my element. The family I've always wanted.'

'You'll have your own, one day.'

A searing pain ripped through her and she hastily lowered her head, unable to bear the joy and hope which lit the darkness of his eyes and turned them into brilliant jet stones.

Max kissed her tightly clenched knuckles and, to her relief, changed the subject abruptly. 'We'll move after lunch. Then, if the weather's at all reasonable, we'll go down to the beach and let off some energy. OK?'

Live every moment.

She flung up her head, tossing away her miseries, and beamed. 'Can't wait!'

'Right, troops,' announced Max, stuffing the last precious item—Fred—into the Range Rover. 'Wag-on-n-n-ns r-r-roll!'

He and Laura broke into a raucous rendition of 'Rawhide'! as he drove down to the head of the bay. Ten minutes earlier he'd been on the phone clinching the purchase of a site in Croydon for another nursery. Max was amazingly versatile, she thought in admiration.

He'd been mysterious about the exact location—or the details—of their rented accommodation, but she knew there were several holiday cottages at the back of Port Gaverne. Most had been converted from the various herring smokeries and the huge fish cellars, where pilchards had once been crushed for their oil.

She didn't care where they all stayed, as long as the accommodation was larger, cleaner, and Max and the children were in it.

'I'm going to exhaust Perran this afternoon,' Max

murmured to her. His hand stole across and caressed her knee. Instantly a flame ignited in the core of her body. 'Ask me why.'

'Why?' she whispered, knowing full well.

'I want a long, uninterrupted evening and night with you. In my arms, on the floor by the fire, then in the library, then by the—'

'Library?'

He grinned, and swung the car suddenly into an entrance. 'Welcome to Pendennis Manor!' Laughing at her astonished face, he leaned over and kissed her directly on the mouth. 'It's rented out in the summer. Vacant most of the winter. For now, it's ours.'

'But...' She paused while he kissed her again. 'It's huge!' she protested.

'Enormous,' he agreed. 'That's why I intend to make full use of every room.'

Perran began kicking the back of her seat. When she turned around, she saw that he was looking excitedly at the cattle in the adjoining field. Beyond that, higher on the hill, she could see sheep grazing.

'Animals too! Perran—there's a donkey with the sheep! Isn't that wonderful? Max, it's going to be heavenly,' she said with a sigh of pleasure. Real domestic bliss.

They unloaded while Perran stood on the post-and-rail fence and ogled the cows. Then he came to help them. By the time everything had been stowed away in the spacious, beautiful house, Kerenza was ready for her sleep. Perran too. He was rubbing his hair and looking drowsy.

'So much for your plans about tonight,' Laura murmured, tucking her nephew up in the big, airy nursery.

'I'm adaptable.' Max sent her a glance of shocking desire, took her hand and led her downstairs. 'Come here,' he said roughly, pulling Laura into his arms.

'The hall?' she cried, her breath short and sharp from his urgency.

'I want you,' he muttered. 'I want you so much it hurts.'

He buried his face in her neck and she sank into his body, sliding her hands up his chest in a gesture of total abandon. Suddenly Max was pressing her hard against the wall, his mouth fierce and demanding, his hands sliding up her legs in frantic haste.

'Max!' she husked, more excited than she could have believed possible.

He silenced her with his mouth. 'I need you,' he muttered. *'Now!'*

His uncontrollable passion, his rapid, hot breathing, his hardness leaping against her immediately set her alight. This was wicked, she thought, quivering in illicit delight at the sharp ache in her body. Broad daylight...

'Laura!' He sounded agonised, his eyes half-closed with desire as he touched, caressed, now moulding one nipple into a peak, then the other, snatching at her clothes as though he couldn't bear to wait.

And nor could she. Small, desperate sounds came from her throat. This was basic hunger. A different kind of sex. Raw, thrilling, instant. She felt herself being lifted, speared sweetly, erotically, their mouths savaging one another, matching the urgent act in unrestrained passion.

She was utterly consumed by him, twisting and writhing, half-crazed in her desperation till they came to a tumultuous climax and Max staggered, somehow regained his balance, and, panting heavily, his eyes glittering like black coals, gently set her on her feet, then swept her into his arms.

It was a long time before their heartbeats subsided. Before Max took a long, shuddering breath and lifted his head. Max kissed her as if he worshipped her, and she felt the tears prick behind her eyes.

He tipped her chin up, his face harrowed. 'You're a witch!' he muttered unsteadily. 'It's getting that I can't keep my hands off you! What are we going to do about that, Laura?'

Shaking, she drew back and rearranged her clothing. Max really had fallen in lust with her. He adored her with his loins, she thought, with unusual waspishness. And would make demands on her...sexy, passionate, unstoppable demands...until someone new came along.

'Glue your palms together,' she said, avoiding the issue entirely.

He took her head in his hands and crushed her mouth beneath his in a sweet, urgent kiss that left her weak and vulnerable.

Then they sat together in the drawing room, silently gazing out at the sinisterly dark cliffs and sparkling sea, each with their own private thoughts.

The gale had died down. Black-backed gulls were wheeling, the sun was shining. Yet Laura was filled with foreboding. She and Max had been shockingly desperate in their love-making. They were living with the sword of Damocles over their heads, ready to slip and slice them in two at the snap of its slender thread.

Max's arm tightened fiercely around her, almost to the point of pain. She turned and drew his mouth down to hers, kissing him as hard as she could in an effort to release the tensions gathering inside her like a threatening storm.

Gently he pushed her away. Looking dazed, he said hoarsely, 'I'm going to stamp about and wake Perran or we'll lose the best part of the afternoon. Get stuff ready for the beach.'

They wandered down the withy lane like any normal family. Man, woman, baby in its buggy, excited four-

year-old plunging into hedges and banks, finding worms
and other exciting objects to be admired.

Laura could hardly breathe for the tautness of her
strained nerves. She left Max to haul the buggy over the
pebbles, sand and rocks, and ran to the edge of the water,
racing back and squealing when the waves rushed back
at her.

She looked back. Max had parked the sleeping
Kerenza safely, and Perran was sitting on a rock, watching her. Frantic to unwind some of her nervous energy,
she ran at the sea again—and then Max's hand was in
hers and they were scurrying back together, screeching
like delirious children as the waves chased them.

Over and over again they played 'dare the sea', ca-
vorting around crazily till Laura was weak from laughter
and the stitch in her side, and had to bend double to
relieve it.

'Perran thinks we're mad,' she gasped breathily, eyeing the solemn little boy still atop the rock.

'Not surprised. I can imagine he's amazed. I never did
this either, when I was a child. My father...' Max
paused, then grabbed Laura's arm. 'I've got it!' he cried.
'Perran doesn't play like a normal child, does he? He
didn't know what to do with his farm animals, other than
make them fight; he wasn't interested in drawing till you
showed him how to do a parrot.'

She smiled. 'He loves Fred. Nuzzles up to him, does
his feed and water... He's very gentle, too. Fred's been
good for him. He loves all animals, Max.'

'I know. He's been badly looked after. No wonder he
was a handful. He's like me.'

She straightened slowly, her eyes wary. 'Like...you?'

'Yes. Deprived. My parents didn't do the usual things
with Daniel and me. We were kept in strict isolation
from the village children. Until I went to prep school I

didn't know half the things a child should about playing. It's possible that Daniel's repeated that with his own son. And Fay, well, she has no idea about children, has she?'

'So…'

'He needs help. Hang on!' he shouted back at her, already halfway to the rock.

And soon Perran was running from the waves, clutching both their hands, being lifted into the air in squealing delight. Finally they were all caught and soaked, and Laura was amazed at his joy, her smile meltingly sweet at the sight of his little face alive with happiness.

Shattered, Max and Laura collapsed on the sand. Once Max had told Perran how to explore the rock pools without harming the purple sea anemones, crabs and shrimps, they left him to make his own discoveries.

Laura listened to the evocative sound of the seabirds and watched cormorants and guillemots diving from the tumble of rocks at the end of the Main. She dreaded going back to London.

'We'll teach him so much,' Max said suddenly, his expression enthusiastic. 'Tomorrow we'll get a kite and take it on the Main. Scare the seagulls a bit! Perhaps we could get him a kitten. A rabbit, too. By the time he goes to school—'

'Max,' she said, stopping him before he went too far. 'Remember the situation.'

He went unnaturally still. Suddenly he got up and walked over to Perran, picking him up and throwing him high in the air, then hugging him tightly as if he never wanted to let him go again. It made Laura's heart turn over. Unable to watch, she searched for a suitable stone and began drawing in the sand.

Perran. Kerenza. Max…

A pair of wet trainers, attached to a pair of sea-stained jeans, stood on the huge pair of eyebrows she'd given her Max. Then their owner knelt and with his finger drew a Laura, cheek to cheek with the Max like two lovers.

A wave washed over the drawings, obliterating them. She and Max stood in the ankle-deep water unheeding, their eyes locked in pain.

'I—I expect Kerenza's awake,' she said chokily. 'I'll take her for a walk.'

He nodded, his eyes never leaving her as she dragged the buggy up to the road which curved around the bay. When she was on the headland, she stole a look back at the beach and he was still where she'd left him, Perran tugging impatiently at his hand. And then she turned away and couldn't look again.

When she returned, it was with a determination to eat, drink, love and be merry. She shut out the image of lemmings, running excitedly to their doom, and pretended that she was on top of the world.

Bathtime was hilarious, the bedtime story even more so, with Laura acting out the parts of the animals that appeared and producing a special, ridiculous voice for each one. It was because she dreaded being alone with Max.

'OK,' she said, jamming the duvet tightly up to Perran's chin, 'Move and you're in for a tickle.' He moved. She tickled. Then kissed him and went over to snuggle her face into Kerenza's. 'Night, darlings,' she said fondly. 'I love you both so very, very much.' And, unable to speak for the choking lump in her throat, she left Max there.

When he came down, her nose was stuck in a large volume on insect life.

'That's a bit beyond the call of duty,' he observed, 'mugging up on the names of everything Perran might bring you to identify.'

'I'm studying zoology,' she said, frowning at a weird

diagram of a beetle's flight patterns. 'I'm miles behind so it's your turn to get supper.'

'Impressive. Why zoology?' he asked, perching on the arm of her chair.

'I do voluntary work at an animal rescue centre every weekend—'

'Get a lot of battered beetles, do you?' he enquired.

She glared. 'Loads.'

'Mugged moths, distressed dragonflies?'

'Oh, put a sock in it!' she complained. 'You can't choose to do only dogs and cats and rabbits—'

'And lions?' His eyes gleamed. 'Elephants?'

She gave him a playful slap and kept her haughty expression. 'In zoology, you have to do it all. I'm up to insects. Leave me in peace.'

'All right. I know my place. Kitchen, kisses, catching.'

'Catching?' She frowned, looking up.

'Supper. I'll go hunt a buffalo or two.' He exited, but she was sure she caught him murmuring, 'Crushed cockroaches...'

She giggled. He was a wonderful tonic when she felt depressed. 'Old MacDonald Had A Farm' was drifting from the hallway. 'Idiot!' she called. He shut the front door, but she could still hear him ee-i-ee-i-o-ing.

Some time later, she realised she hadn't turned a single page, and gave up. 'Kisses, couch potato,' she said contentedly to herself, and switched on the TV.

When Max came in again, she was sobbing her eyes out.

'Darling!' he cried in alarm, setting down the tray he'd been carrying. His arms came around her and she struggled to be free.

'Shh!' she sniffed furiously. Her head craned far to one side. 'Max, out of the *way*! I can't *see*!'

Stunned, he turned to see the last few frames of *Love Story*. 'Well, I'll be...'

The credits rolled and Laura howled her eyes out. 'It's s-o-o lovely!' she wept.

'Oh, Laura!' he said with deep affection. 'I do love you so much.'

Her tears dried in an instant and she blinked in confusion. 'Wh-what did you say?' she gasped.

Max collected the tray. Solemnly he put a plate in front of Laura. 'Supper,' he said. 'Buffaloes are off on Thursdays, so it's only fish and chips from the local, but...'

Her lip quivered. The words 'I love you' had been spelled out in chips. Max really knew the way to her heart. Better than red roses and the serious formality of a dinner somewhere. She adored his off the wall approach. Chips! He'd laugh her into bed once more.

'Oh, don't start crying again!' he said in mock exasperation. 'I'm not trying to starve you! You can actually have more chips *and* a piece of fish, but they were superfluous to my statement so I piled them all on my plate. Well, what do you have to say?'

Laughing, crying, unable to comprehend what this meant, she said, 'Give me my share!'

He did. Long, lingering kisses.

'My supper's getting cold!' she said weakly.

'It'll heat up. Laura, I love you. I adore you. I don't know what happened to us before, but I sure as hell don't want to lose you again. I think I'd jump off a cliff if I thought there was that possibility—'

'Don't say that!' she cried quickly. Her fingers touched his mouth, drifting over the sensual curves. 'Not even in jest.'

'Then put me out of my misery.' He knelt on the floor,

took her hand in his and looked deeply into her eyes. 'Marry me, Laura. Marry me and we'll be happy for the rest of our lives; I promise you.'

CHAPTER SEVEN

Too late. Five years, one lost baby and her ruined body too late. Life could be so cruel.

Max was offering her everything she wanted and she'd have to turn him down. Her heart was breaking all over again. Why her? Why should she be the one to be torn apart and put back together only to be ripped in two again?

'Don't look so shattered, sweetheart,' he said, smiling affectionately. 'Think of the fun we'll have together. Like this, but a hundred times more meaningful. And it'll go on for ever. We're made for one another. We do great harmonies when we sing.'

'Max—'

'Wait a minute. I haven't finished coaxing you yet.'

He grinned, and her heart turned over. He was so happy that it hurt.

'I have a confession,' he told her gently. 'I deceived you at our meeting the other day.'

'How?' she asked warily.

'When Daniel asked me to get you to look after the children, I decided to make things difficult for you, because you'd hurt my pride. So I planned from the beginning to go along with you too. Maybe I couldn't have you—but I'd show you what it felt like to want someone and have them walk away. Then...after a few minutes...my old feelings surged back as if we'd never been apart. I fell in love with you all over again.'

She glared from beneath dark brows, gathered together like storm clouds. Anger welled up inside her. Why did he have to love her?

Laura's eyes flashed. This had to stop. Now.

'You can't possibly love—'

'I cook a mean shepherd's pie and I can get seeds out of your hair,' he said, ignoring her completely. 'You make everywhere untidy; I clear up. You cry over soppy films and make wonderful cut-out men from newspaper. That's grounds enough for me. Now, about this wedding. You'll get one of those white meringue things to wear and walk down the aisle, and as a concession I'll agree to us leaving on an elephant—'

'Stop it, Max! How *could* you?!' she raged, a tight mass of fury.

Max's mouth dropped open. 'W-h-a-t?'

'We have *days* ahead of us! They could have been so perfect and—and you go and spoil them by *proposing*!'

'Laura,' he cried in astonishment. 'I thought—'

'No, you didn't!' she yelled, stamping her foot and knocking the plate of 'I love you' chips to the floor. Max stared at them blankly. 'You're only asking me,' she went on hysterically, 'because we've had fun and all this mummies and daddies stuff has come close to some ideal image you have about families—'

'Yes! Damn right I am!' he bit out. 'What's wrong with that? *We* could be like this in *our* lives. Dammit, Laura, those chips were supposed to melt your heart!'

He was deeply hurt. Already there was a tightening of his facial muscles, a new wariness in his dark velvet eyes. She wanted to kiss him and give him whatever he wanted, because it hurt her to hurt him. But she couldn't marry him, knowing she could never give him children.

Desperately thinking of a way out of this without upsetting him, she muttered foolishly, 'They—they were lovely—'

'Don't patronise me!' His brows snapped together as if he meant business. 'I'm asking you to marry me, not award me marks out of ten for technique. You want roses, I'll give you a roomful. Champagne; I'll fill the bath. I just thought you liked surprises. Laughing. I thought you'd find my approach novel. Funny.'

Despite the angry tone she wanted to say yes with all her heart. It took every ounce of self-control to look him in the eyes and say gently, 'No, Max.'

In an exasperated, jerky movement, he rose from his knees and began to pace up and down the room with hard, angry strides as if a thousand devils were struggling inside his body, driving him on.

'We're a fantastic team. We work brilliantly together—'

'Max, marriage isn't something you go into because you get major points on a checklist—'

'Shut up!' he roared. 'I'm having my say. And then you can explain why the hell you don't think we'd be happy for the rest of our lives. I love you. I feel totally at ease with you—and yet crazily aroused whenever I touch you, look at you... Like now. I want you now. I want you about every eight seconds on average.' He shot her a thunderous look. 'You see? I'm risking everything—my pride, my personal feelings, all my dark, inner secrets—'

'Don't!' she whispered, appalled.

'Why? I don't understand, Laura!' Seething with anger, Max strode over and hauled her to her feet. 'Have I read the messages wrongly? I thought you loved me too. Are you like this with every man you meet? Friendly, open, funny, affectionate—? Oh, hell!' he cursed, his face contorted in anguish. 'Is that just the way you are? Do you adore sex? Do you sleep with all men as readily as you slept with me?'

'No, Max!' Horrified, she wriggled, wincing in pain as his hands clamped more tightly around her arms. 'Let me go!' she spat.

'Not yet. Not till you tell me something.' He grabbed

her jaw and she was forced to look into his merciless eyes. 'Were you lying to me about Luke? You carry his card around with you...'

'To phone him!' she protested. 'I have to phone him—'

'At the shop, surely?' he persisted savagely. 'Not at his home—'

'I swear to you, he isn't the reason!' Her eyes implored him to leave her alone.

His grip eased. She rubbed her arms with an accusing expression, and he seemed about to apologise when he turned, pushed a distracted hand through his hair and took a few steps in one direction, then another, as if he didn't know what to do with himself.

Laura watched, distraught, twisting her hands till the skin felt sore. Finally he ended up at the French doors, dragged back the drapes with an angry gesture that almost ripped them from the pole and flung the doors open, stumbling out onto the sheltered terrace.

Somehow she managed to stand up. To walk unsteadily to the open doors. The air was chilly, but she was already cold and bloodless, as if all the life had been sucked from her, so it didn't matter.

Max had his back to her, his head bent. Her instincts were to put her arms around him, and she had to fight to stop herself from giving him any hint or encouragement.

So, cold, frigid, as miserable as she'd ever been, she merely stood there, knowing she had to make him understand they could never get together.

Even though it was what she longed for with every crashing, jerking beat of her aching heart.

'I like Luke a lot,' she said, her voice cracking with the strain. 'But that doesn't mean I fall into his arms whenever the shop's empty. If you really want to know, Max,' she went on, determined that he shouldn't think of her as an easy lay, 'I haven't made love to anyone else but you.'

His shoulders tensed then began to heave with the pressure of his fast, hard breathing. He grabbed the post supporting the veranda, and Laura noticed that white bone showed through his knuckles.

'No one...but me.'

She bit her lip. That had been a mistake. It hinted that she'd never got over him. 'I think you have an apology to make to me,' she said, anxious to divert him.

She didn't know how to handle this. Only the truth would satisfy him and she shrank from that.

'I'm sorry,' he said curtly, and she had to strain to hear. He lifted his head and stared out into the darkness, the fist at his side clenched so tightly it quivered noticeably.

'It's not like you to be jealous,' she ventured.

'No.' He inhaled harshly. 'I can't believe how sick I feel when I think of you giving yourself to someone else. I felt like beating Luke's face to a pulp. It's irrational and ugly, I know, and I hate and despise myself for it. But I'm not sane where you're concerned.'

'Better I get out of your way, then,' she forced out.

As if compelled to move by the pent-up energy in his body, he suddenly whirled, his vehemence virtually pinning her to the spot.

'You don't get it, do you? I can't face the thought of living without you!'

Laura gazed at him in horror. 'You can't meant that, Max!'

'Every time I think of it,' he seethed, 'it's like a pain scything me in half! I don't want this ever to end.'

'It must—'

'I won't let it! You haven't given me one good reason for refusing to marry me. Don't you long to live in Cornwall?'

'Yes, but—'

'I know how you respond to me. I look at you and you light up. It's the same for me!' he flung angrily. 'Now give me a decent excuse, one I can believe in!'

Laura shrank back in fear. In the darkness, all she could see was the glint in his eyes. He meant to bully her till he had the information he wanted.

Half the truth, then.

'All right.' Laura licked her dry lips. Her eyes were huge with fear. She had to tell him enough...but not all. 'I—I was willing to forget the past for the children's sakes. Because of their needs, I accepted you unconditionally—'

'What the devil do you mean?' he growled menacingly. 'What past? The way you dumped me? Are you suggesting that it was my fault?'

'You know damn well it was!' she cried hotly. 'How can you pretend otherwise?'

She was beside herself with anger. He had no right to make her take the blame for what had happened!

'Tell me,' he muttered sarcastically, 'how I dumped you. How it was my fault. I'm fascinated to know what I did.'

Laura lifted an obstinate face, shaking with fury that he was too arrogant, too preciously wonderful to consider himself in the wrong.

'Your parents were right,' she said coldly. 'You never admit to mistakes. You sweep through life assuming that everyone else is to blame for disasters.'

'What the devil did I do?' he shouted.

'Other women!' she yelled back. 'Oh, yes, you might well look shocked! I know, you see! That's why I couldn't ever marry you. I couldn't trust you to be faithful. Women are too attractive to you—and they sure as hell find you irresistible! Well, you may find it macho and amusing to be fickle, but I don't. In my family we stay faithful. You'll have to find someone else, who doesn't mind you stringing along a load of mistresses cosied up in apartments in the capitals of the world.' Her voice rose with her misery and rage. 'Personally,' she shouted, 'I'm not into time-share!'

He came towards her and she backed away, but her progress was halted by a wall. He slammed his hands on either side of her head so hard that it must have hurt, because the shock ran through his arms in a wave. But none of that registered on his face as he leaned close and began to speak.

'Listen, and listen good,' he hissed. 'I... have...never...ever...two-timed *anyone*! Got that? Slow enough, clear enough for you?' he raged.

But he was lying. Must be. She stood her ground. 'You still won't admit it, will you? What about your fiancée?' she countered.

She was close to weeping in frustration and disappointment. He was a coward. Less than a man for not owning up. Her Max...fallen off the pedestal again.

'My *who*?' he rasped impatiently.

'The one from Surrey, the one you kept quiet while you were fooling around with me!' she flung.

'I *never* fooled around with you,' he growled, his brows lowered furiously over his hot black eyes. 'And I don't know what you mean... Surrey? I don't know any-one—'

'Stop lying, Max!' she cried, her voice vibrating with emotion. 'Your parents told me all about her.'

'My parents!' He stepped back, and she felt she could breathe again. For a moment he stood there in absolute silence, examining her face intently. 'My parents.' The edge had been taken off his anger. He sounded...defeated. Perhaps, thought Laura, he knew he couldn't keep up the pretence any longer. 'When?' he demanded stonily. 'Tell me exactly what happened.'

If that was what it took...

She met his eyes defiantly. 'The day after you went to France they came round to see me. They explained about your fiancée and apologised on your behalf. They were very kind and concerned—and distinctly uncomfortable. Your mother kept glancing anxiously at your father and stumbling over her words—'

'I bet she did,' muttered Max viciously.

'They were terribly ashamed of your behaviour...' she began, her face indignant.

'No. Ashamed of theirs.' His mouth was bitter as he took in her bewilderment, her wary suspicion.

'I don't know what you're talking about,' she said sullenly. 'But you can see why I didn't want anything to do with you. I don't want to be involved with a man who has so few decent values in life. I won't be treated with contempt, Max!'

He threw back his head and groaned. When he looked at her again, it was with gentle affection.

'Don't you understand, sweetheart?' He sighed when she shook her head dumbly. So he took her limp, cold hand in his. 'They invented a fiancée for me. She never existed.'

'Why would they lie?' she demanded, disappointed by his evasion.

'They didn't approve of you,' he answered gently. 'You were from the village. A nobody. My father expected me to marry someone well-connected.'

'He didn't stop us going around together,' she reminded him sharply.

The General had been distant, but polite. No hostility at all. Max was lying again. Sickness filled her stomach, and she snatched her hand away, wrapping her arms around herself in misery.

'Why should he have? As far as he was concerned, you were only someone I was trying my teeth on. Something to play with,' Max said caustically. 'Your father had only been a fisherman. Your mother worked in the post office. He didn't see as far as his nose where they were concerned. Didn't recognise your father's loyalty, love for his fellow man, his courage, or your mother's battle to keep a home together for you and your sister. He didn't see what I saw…and envied.

'Anyway, as I was about to board the plane, I asked my father to keep an eye on you. I think he knew then that I was serious. He soon knocked that on the head, though, didn't he? He conjured up a fiancée for me where none existed.'

'I have to take your word for that, don't I? But there was Fay!' Her eyes narrowed when he looked puzzled. 'You can't forget that!' she declared. 'Your affair with her lasted for five months! How do you think I felt, hearing a blow-by-blow account about it from my own sister? You came back early from France and missed me so much that you jumped straight into her bed! You didn't even try to contact me—'

'*Fay*? Laura, what kind of man do you think I am?'

'A philanderer!' she all but sobbed.

'You're nowhere near the truth! First, I did try to find you. Second, Fay's a renowned flirt. She'd been with most of the good-looking lads in the village by the time she was seventeen,' he said in disgust.

'That's why I hated you for going with her! Fay's beautiful and I'm so plain—'

'Whoa. Fay's superficially attractive. You have the kind of quiet beauty that creeps up on you and hits you in the solar plexus and knots you up till you can't breathe. You—'

'Now you're patronising me,' she whispered, appalled that he could be so cruel.

'I mean everything I say,' he told her grimly. 'I came back early because I hadn't heard from you and I was worried. Your mother clammed up. I talked to Fay, hoping she might tell me where you'd gone—'

'She—she said you'd gone out together,' Laura mumbled.

'Then she's a liar!' he said indignantly. 'Did your mother make any mention of this?'

'No. But she wouldn't have wanted to hurt me. You…you took Fay on long drives. Dinner. I got a rundown of the menus. You made love in the hay field, your car…everywhere! She said…'

'That's all imaginary.'

'But…' Too upset to go on, she stared unhappily at Max, totally confused.

'You honestly believed I could behave like that?' he asked, after a long, cold silence.

'You were besotted. It was the hottest affair…'

He grunted. 'She tried to make it one and I rejected her. Fay doesn't like rejection. It had never crossed her path before. She paid me back by refusing to say where you were, and turned her mind to seducing Daniel. That's why I was against the wedding. I knew she was marrying him for the wrong reasons. Though I was mistaken, as it turned out. They had fallen in love, it seems. She likes to control him; he likes to be controlled.'

'I don't know what to think!' Laura put a trembling hand to her mouth.

'How can I convince you? I could swear on the Bible and I'm not sure you'd trust me. You've got an inferiority complex where Fay's concerned. If you could only see that you're more beautiful, more lovable… Goddammit, Fay hasn't even got a sense of humour!'

'She—she said you couldn't…wanted…' Stumbling over her words, she fought to sort them out. 'You couldn't get enough of her,' she finished in a small voice.

'Then she's a vicious, vindictive, malicious, jealous

woman and I feel nothing but contempt for her,' he said furiously. 'Remember,' he went on, 'what I told you about your father? The influence he'd had on me?'

'Y-e-s, but—'

'You know I wanted to be a man like him. Someone with integrity. Does it sound likely that I'd act like a prat and play fast and loose when the woman I loved was waiting for me?' He came close again, his soft breath whispering over her agonised face. 'You know in your heart of hearts the kind of man I am. Listen to your instincts. I've been totally faithful to you all these years.'

She couldn't dare to believe that. Because... Unwilling to reach the obvious conclusion, she jerked out, 'You're telling me you...you never made love to Fay...not once...*ever*?'

'Never! Dammit, Laura, you know what a liar your sister is! Do you honestly imagine I'd sleep with a promiscuous, shallow little madam like her? What do I have to do? Slice an artery and write a denial in my life's blood?'

She was almost choking on the cruel truth. Fay had lied to her! Laura drove her nails into her palms, desperate to conquer the bile which rose in her churning stomach.

'I believe you.' In a daze, she spoke aloud what had been going round and round in her mind. 'Perran isn't your son!'

'What was that?' Max said sharply.

Laura's hand went to her mouth, but it was too late. 'Nothing—'

The blaze of his eyes cut her off. 'Who said Perran was mine? Fay?' When she nodded, he ground his teeth in anger. 'That sister of yours needs beating! And so do you,' he muttered, 'for believing her.'

'The timing was right!' she cried. 'According to Fay, you and she had been having this affair for almost five

months. That's when she told me about it, when I—'
Laura stopped herself just in time. Max must never know
she'd been five months pregnant. 'When I knew,' she
corrected. 'I suppose she couldn't tell me it wasn't your
baby, because that would make her out to be a liar.'

'An odd situation. You, coming to look after your
sister's child, with an ex-lover you thought was his father.' His tone was bitter, his eyes reproachful. 'No wonder you were uptight.'

'But...why would she do this to me, Max?' she asked
piteously.

'Jealousy.'

Stunned, Laura was beginning to realise the implica-
tions. Perran was Daniel's child.

She felt as though she'd been hit by a thunderbolt.
Max had been blameless. First his parents had made her
doubt him. Then Fay. Laura felt her stomach lurch.
She'd chosen to believe them because she couldn't
imagine that Max might really love her.

And it was Fay, with her gloating news that Max was
a tiger in bed, with the revelation that she, Fay, was now
pregnant with his child, who had caused Laura to lose
her baby. She felt faint.

She needn't have lost Max or her baby at all.

Frozen into immobility, she heard him dimly in the
background, upbraiding her, clearly affronted by her lack
of faith.

Get me out of this nightmare! she moaned, her eyes
closed in agony. My *sister*...

'Always jealous of you,' Max was saying grimly.
'People loved you for your own sake. She had nothing
to offer but her body; that's what made her popular with
the boys...'

His words floated away to be dominated by her own
horrified thoughts. Her own flesh and blood, her sister,

had torn apart her world, sent her into the depths of despair, ripped from her everything she'd adored!

It was inconceivable. But horribly true.

She swayed. No wonder Fay had avoided her after the miscarriage. She must have known what she'd done, what it had meant, physically, mentally, emotionally, for Laura to have lost…no. Not lost. That was an inadequate word for what had happened. Destroyed. Max's baby, dead inside her. Harsh words. Cruel. Brutal.

'You'd never see that,' Max went on relentlessly. 'You believed everyone to be perfect, especially your sister. But it was *she* who corrupted Daniel and persuaded him that a life on the road would be fun. She who hated responsibility. She who made sure he and I never met again, so God knows what lies she told him about me. It was she who was carrying the drugs when they were arrested—'

'No!' she cried in a weak croak.

'Believe it!' Max's angry eyes captured hers. 'Your sister—and, yes, my parents—caused this trouble between us. We now have an opportunity to change the situation—'

'*No! No, no, no!*'

Unable to bear it any longer, she pushed past him and ran across the terrace, knocking over a rattan chair and a glass-topped table in her frantic dash. She crashed into a bush and came to a halt, shuddering, incapable of crying because there was nothing inside her.

'You'll hurt yourself.' Max's voice, gruff, deep.

I already have, she thought piteously.

'What are you afraid of?' he demanded.

'I want you to leave me alone.' She trembled when he put his hands on her fragile shoulders and she felt the weight, the heat of him like a burden she'd carry for ever.

The irony of it. He'd loved her. He had longed for a

family. He'd been ready for commitment, had tried to find her...

The dreams could all have been hers. Dear God! Would this heartache ever end? How long would she go on castigating herself, her sister, life itself, for dealing her such a cruel hand?

'Because?'

She snapped. 'Oh, for heaven's sake!' she yelled, whipping around in a wild movement. 'I don't want to marry you! It's—it's been fun,' she said, angry because she knew she must reject him convincingly, the words rushing out like a river in full spate before she could change her mind. 'But we can't turn the clock back. I can't change my feelings—'

'I thought you loved me,' he said thickly. 'Tell me you don't! Look me in the eyes and tell me straight!'

Somehow she did. 'Love you?' she cried, the hysteria bubbling dangerously close to the surface. 'Whatever gave you that idea? I lark about with everyone. You know that. Get a life! Take no for an answer, will you?'

She was aware of him stiffening in shock. But she continued to glare at him, forcing him to go, needing his hatred.

She couldn't marry him. And she couldn't tell him why. She loved him too much.

It would devastate him to know that his baby had died. In this mood he was unpredictable. He might do anything, his passions were riding so high. There was a hard, ruthless side to Max that frightened her. Far better that he believed she didn't care enough, and that he was free...free to marry someone else.

Her face went white with the pang of jealousy and misery which seared viciously through her body, her cheekbones standing out taut and hard as she contained her feelings.

'That's it, then?'

She winced at the curt, hard, clipping finality of each word. 'Yes,' was all she could manage.

He walked back into the house without a word. But every bone in his body, every muscle, every fibre all were saying one thing to her.

I wash my hands of you, now and for ever.

CHAPTER EIGHT

LAURA dragged herself up to bed. Max had gone out. She slept alone. No—she tossed restlessly, thoughts filling her head mercilessly, taunting her with the terrible truth.

Her sister had acted shamefully, and Laura's only consolation was that her parents weren't around to know. Over and over again the facts repeated themselves in her head.

She could now have been a wife and mother. Max's wife.

Stuffing her knuckles into her mouth, she curled up into a tight ball of misery.

Too shocked to cry. Motionless. Numb. Tormented by her thoughts which wouldn't leave her alone, like a tape loop playing a maddening tune.

'Are you awake?' Max. Cold, humiliated, offended Max.

Of course she was! she wanted to scream. How could her mind ever be at peace again?

She remained where she was, every single muscle clenched to stop herself from hurling herself at him, begging him to love her, no matter what...or attacking him with fists, feet, nails. Love, hate, she felt them both, and it was taking all her will-power to hold those feelings back.

He snapped on the light. 'We must get a few things sorted before the children awake.'

'Like what?' she muttered uncooperatively, irritated by his curt, matter-of-fact common sense.

'How we behave to one another in front of them.' He came to sit on the end of the bed.

Laura closed her eyes. He was right. They'd have to act normally. How could she do that? Appalled, she slowly wriggled around and sat up. It was gone three in the morning.

Max looked as if he'd been out all night, his eyes defeated and drooping with sleep, a dark stubble on his face, and no life in his expression or his voice at all.

He wore only the jumper, shirt and jeans he'd had on that evening, and a cold dampness was coming off his clothes as if he'd walked in the mist, or had been lying on damp grass.

'You look frozen,' she said, wide-eyed with anxiety.

His eyes flickered with contempt. 'I am. Does it matter?'

'I—I don't want you to be ill,' she said wretchedly.

'That's the least of my problems.'

She hated to see him like this. He was speaking in a cold, indifferent way, as though they were strangers, but his eyes betrayed him. He'd been deeply hurt. He'd offered her his love and she'd thrown it back in his face.

Her hand stretched out before she knew. 'Max...' she began huskily.

He leapt up from the bed as if she'd offered him poison. 'Don't play with my emotions!' he snarled, crushing her sympathy with one glance from his ferocious eyes. 'Stop thinking about your own needs! Hell, Laura, I thought you were different. Maybe you and Fay *are* alike—'

'No!' she said hotly. 'I was only—'

'Well, don't ''only''!' he bit out. 'Save it for when we're with the children. I don't want them to know there's hostility between us.'

'Hostility...! No. Of course,' she agreed numbly.

'They're in a fragile state. I don't want Perran regressing. Agreed?'

'Yes, but how—?'

'We'll keep up a front.' Max glowered at her. 'That means remembering how we were.' His mouth thinned. 'Laughter. Fooling around. Having fun.' He looked at her steadily, projecting a deep dislike. 'Touching.'

'T-touching?' She gulped.

He seemed to be enjoying her dismay. 'I seem to remember we did a lot of that,' he drawled, his eyes veiled now. 'For Perran's sake, we're going to be as fond of each other as ever. Play your part well. Or you'll destroy him.'

Laura shuddered, and then gasped when Max began to shed his jumper. 'What...?' She licked her lips. 'What are you doing?'

'Getting into bed. I'm bushed.' He flipped open the buttons of his shirt, his gaze mocking her undisguised alarm.

Laura's mouth opened and then shut again. 'Perran's not here,' she said, jerking out each word in short, frightened bursts. 'There are other bedrooms! You don't have to keep up appearances now, this minute!'

The shirt was discarded, revealing his broad, beautiful chest. Her eyes feasted deliriously on the touchable skin for a moment before she remembered that he was off-limits.

'He'll expect to find us in bed together.' Max's fingers began loosening his belt.

'Asleep,' she said, nodding so vigorously she thought her neck might snap.

'Asleep, awake...'

His jeans slithered to the floor. He reached for the waistband of his briefs, and she dived under the duvet, her whole body throbbing with hunger.

'You're not touching me!' she cried in panic.

She was rolled back, and found herself inches from a pair of inky-dark eyes spitting fire at her.

'After what I've learnt about you?' He gave an insulting laugh.

Disappointment and relief hit her at the same time. Confused, she tried to make sense of her battling desires.

'How long before you release me from this vile situation, Max?' she breathed, terrified by the bitter anger in his eyes. 'How long do we keep up this farce?'

His hand drifted to her throat and she held her breath. 'Till Perran speaks.'

'That could be...ages!' she wailed.

'I care about my nephew more than our collapsed, non-existent relationship,' he grated. 'You're not important any more. He is. That child isn't going to suffer the mistakes of his parents—even if we have to play-act for a month.'

'No, not a month,' she cried in agitation. 'I couldn't, my work—'

'To hell with your work!' Max said grimly. 'Is that more vital than a child's mental state?'

'Of course not!'

'Speak to Luke. Explain the situation. Last time you rang he said his sister was coping brilliantly.'

'With a stand-in like that, I could lose my job,' she muttered.

'You won't have any trouble getting another. You're too good a baker for that. You *know* we have to help Perran. We can't hire a nanny for him. You agreed that another change would be detrimental at this moment.' Something bitter and painful distorted his face. 'I love the children. But I'm not exactly thrilled about staying here with you,' he said cuttingly. 'Like it or not, we have no choice.'

She fell silent, dreading the thought of Max sleeping

with her, hating her, pretending to be merry and bright day after day... It would be awful.

'I'll get him to talk soon,' she said faintly.

'Do that.'

He left her abruptly, and she shut her eyes till the rustling sounds stopped and the light went out. Max got into bed and settled down, his back to her.

For a long time Laura lay there, stiff and as rigid as a poker, listening to his shallow breathing. He didn't sleep either; she knew that because she'd learnt the sounds and signs of his body so well. His breathing always deepened and slowed, his body relaxed and he gave a little unconscious sigh of pleasure. This time he stayed motionless and tense.

The urge to get up and leave was overwhelming, but she stuck it out, focusing her mind on how to break Perran's silence. Perhaps they would have to see a psychologist. But she sensed that Max had been right all along, that her nephew needed stability and love and routine. Perran needed to be played with, too.

Curse the happy families! She didn't know how she could stand it. Well, she'd had enough of lying there, moping, worrying. There was a glimmer of light coming through the curtains, and she needed to get away from Max before she started smashing things.

Without bothering to be quiet, she swung her legs out of the bed and stood up.

Max immediately twisted around. 'What's the matter—is one of the children crying?' he asked groggily.

'I'm going for a walk.'

Tight-lipped, she stumbled in the gloom to the chest containing her underwear and banged against it, knocking her shin. A cut-glass jug of water teetered on the marble top and she watched it in surprise as it fell, smashing to smithereens and scattering shards all over her bare feet.

'Damn!'

Typical, she thought, glaring at the glittering pieces. Everything she planned went contrary on her. Something got smashed after all.

'Stay where you are!' Max warned.

She started at his sharp intervention, and glared. He was getting out of bed. Her eyes locked on his tight, naked buttocks, the lean, narrow waist...

'I can manage perfectly—'

'Do as you're told!' he barked, reaching, mercifully, for his towelling robe and Moroccan leather slip-ons. He turned on the light. 'You move an inch and you'll cut your feet.'

'I have. A bit. Nothing dramatic. I'll live.' She peered down, watching small specks of blood coming from a minuscule cut on the arch of her foot.

'Wait.'

'Thanks,' she muttered.

'Don't mention it. I don't want the carpet ruined.'

'Oh, pardon me for bleeding!' she snapped bitchily, covering up her disappointment that he cared only for the wretched Axminster.

He looked at her as if she'd sworn in church, and she blushed. 'That's not like you, Laura,' he commented in disapproval.

'You don't know me, then,' she flung.

'Apparently not.'

He strode from the room. His bare feet could be heard padding down the stairs. Laura waited, imprisoned by the glass, her mouth sullen because she hated herself for her sour outburst. Max was turning her into a prize cow.

When he returned, bearing a plastic bag, a dustpan and brush and the first-aid box, she'd picked up an emery board and was pretending to be fixated with achieving a symmetric curve on each nail.

'How on earth did you knock the jug over?' he asked

in exasperation, dabbing at the cut. It stopped bleeding, and he turned his attention to the glass.

'Easily,' she said crossly, watching him painstakingly removing the tiny slivers from her feet and in between her toes. 'I'm clumsy.'

'Only when you're agitated.'

Surprised by his remark, she looked down on his dark head and wondered if that was true. Without realising, her eyes softened. He was carefully picking the last few pieces off her wet feet, his lashes lowered, mouth pursed in concentration.

And she'd never wanted him, loved him more.

She let out a low moan before she knew it was there.

'Damn!' Max scowled at a cut which had appeared across his thumb, oozing dark blood.

And, again before she knew what she was doing, she had flung the emery board away, crouched down on her haunches and taken his thumb into her mouth. Her eyes half closed when she tasted the blood, and she quivered at the feel of his thumb between her lips, touching the roof of her mouth, filling her tastebuds with the sweetness of his warm flesh...

He muttered something—like a curse, a groan, a plea—she wasn't sure, only that he had lifted her up in his arms. Her gaze flew to his face and she opened her eyes wide. A hard and angry desire had tautened his cheekbones and stretched his cruel mouth so that his lips were parted, his teeth bared.

'Don't!' she whimpered, scared by the darkness of his expression.

But he dropped her on the bed. Rolled up her nightdress as she struggled silently, and dragged it over her head.

'Sure?' he asked thickly.

Laura nodded, petrified. Then he touched her breast,

and her eyes closed, her body arching to him at once, betraying her.

'Sure?' He was mocking her, licking each tense nipple into a painfully engorged peak, and her hips were writhing beneath his.

'Don't!'

He kissed her neck, her throat, breasts, every inch of her body. Every inch but her mouth.

Blurring tears filled her eyes. She did want him. She couldn't pretend otherwise—he had found the evidence and was stroking her soft dampness with skilled fingers.

'Kiss me,' she moaned.

Max kissed her silky flat stomach passionately, his stubble gently grazing her flesh and sending tiny ripples of excitement rolling through her entire body.

But, furious at being treated like a whore, Laura grabbed a handful of his hair and hauled him up her body. *'Me!'* she exploded. 'Me!'

He just looked at her cynically, resisting. She found herself shaking, demanding with her body, her eyes, her hands…desperate to share at least some part of him. She tore at his shoulders, struggled to bite, to vent her anger and her misery on him.

Why she did that, she didn't know. She knew only that some uncontainable eruption had occurred inside her and she needed to lash out and give way to her emotions—or crack with the tension.

'No.' With a shocking lack of need, Max flung her away and threw her nightdress at her. 'Get it on. Perran will be awake soon.' His eyes silvered. 'When I said "touching",' he added tightly, 'I didn't mean when we're alone. I'm not here to satisfy your sexual desires, Laura, however ravenous you are.'

Humiliation washed over her. With trembling fingers she fumbled to drag the nightdress over her head. It got stuck. Almost shouting with frustration, she wriggled and twisted in a desperate urge to find the neck opening.

There was a growl from Max. Two hands cupped her breasts. She froze and then gave a low, pained cry. Max had kissed each one, tugged gently at each nipple.

'Leave me alone, you brute!' she yelled, furious with his deliberate torture. 'It was you who started all this, you who threw me on the bed—'

'What do you expect? You had my thumb in your mouth and were looking up at me with those big baby blues, just asking for it!' he seethed. 'If you weren't sending me bedtime messages, what the hell *were* you doing?'

Her head found its way through the tangled folds of cotton and she dragged the nightdress down, her face appearing from it, hot and flushed and angry.

'Applying first aid,' she muttered crossly, not daring to look at him. He was right—and her feelings must have been as clear as if she'd written them in banner headlines and shouted them with a megaphone.

'I think you've been reading the wrong manual,' he told her tightly. 'And if you don't want any more misunderstandings then don't parade yourself so blatantly,' he added with a snarl. 'I'm not made of stone!'

'We're sharing the same bedroom! What do you want me to do, sew myself into a vest?' she yelled.

'A vest would be just perfect,' he said, getting up from the bed and clearly loathing her.

'Max…' She started again, this time without her voice wobbling so much. 'Max, we can't go on like this!'

'No,' he agreed. Frowning down at her, he said coldly, 'It's perfectly simple if we keep to the arrangement, Laura. We are friends during the day and strangers at night. It'll work if you don't try to blur the two. Now you know how easy it would be for us to have sex. Our bodies haven't caught up with the current situation yet.

Put a beautiful, naked and eager woman in my bed and I'm likely to respond. But, under the circumstances, I'd rather we avoided any kind of sexual gratification.' His mouth thinned. 'I prefer to love the women I share my body with.'

Laura winced. It wasn't lust. He was making it sound as if she was on heat. She just loved him.

'Well, don't jump off any cliffs,' she warned. 'I'm not offering you first aid if you do.'

'I'll make a note of that,' he answered caustically.

Flinging back her head in challenge, she locked eyes with him. 'I'm making rules too. Don't play games. We show affection, but there's to be no sly, sexual teasing. No groping. Understood? If you taunt me, if you get your own back on me by foul means, I'll go—and you'll have to solve Perran's problem all on your own. I mean it. That's a promise.'

He grunted. 'I'm going to have a shower.'

Laura suddenly felt flat and wiped out. She slid back under the covers, appalled at the situation. Living a lie. Playing the affectionate partner, knowing that Max now despised and resented her.

But it had to be done. And she'd do her best, exert all her energies in an effort to stabilise her nephew. Then she'd go back to London and her old, empty life.

Too tired to think any more, she let a sleepy nothingness drift over her till she fell heavily asleep, wishing a miracle would happen and she and Max could be happy again.

'Wake up, darling!' murmured Max lovingly, his hand shaking her shoulder gently.

She smiled, half-asleep, her mouth drowsily pouting. 'Mornin' sweethear',' she mumbled.

Two chubby little arms stole around her neck. Her eyes flipped open. 'Oh, Perran, poppet!' she cried in delight. 'Give me a kiss. And another. Mmm! Scrummy!'

Her eyes slanted to Max. Her heart was thudding because she realised he'd been forcing the affection. A hollowness opened up somewhere in her stomach. But if he could do it, so could she.

'Well,' she said brightly as Perran began to trampoline on the bed, 'where to today? A trip in the car and a picnic, Max?'

An ecstatic Perran flung himself into mid-air and Max caught the little boy in his arms, swinging him around. '*Terrific* idea!' he said over-heartily, as if, thought Laura wryly, she'd suggested tea with the Queen, a hit musical and dinner at Claridges to follow. 'Where?'

'I'll think of somewhere while I shower. Check on Kerenza and do her nappy if she needs it, will you…' she licked her dry lips '…darling?' she finished breathily, and hastily grabbed her robe and rushed to the bathroom.

When she came back, Max was dressed in a soft green shirt and matching sweater with honey-coloured chinos. He was cuddling a gurgling Kerenza and playing 'Round and round the garden, like a teddy bear'. Perran wore black cords and his favourite rugby shirt in the colours of Cornwall's team, a searing yellow and black.

'Hello, bumble bee,' she said affectionately, nuzzling his round, stripy tummy.

In delight, he buzzed at her. She flicked a quick, excited glance at Max. It was the first sound, other than laughter, that he had made.

'More like a striped cow,' Max said casually. 'How do cows go, Laura?'

She pretended to frown and ponder. But Perran didn't take the bait. Instead, he dashed around the room with his arms outstretched, being a bee.

'Good try,' she said generously to Max, collecting her clothes.

He nodded and continued his game with Kerenza. She paused, her heart assailed by pangs of love at the dark head bent over the fair. There was something infinitely touching about a strong, very male man absorbed with a tiny baby.

'Wheeeeow!' went Perran, skimming by, grabbing Laura's briefs and putting them on his head.

She laughed and selected another pair. Max exchanged glances with her again, then tucked Kerenza between two pillows and leapt after Perran. Subtly he changed the sound they were making to that of a car's engine. Perran copied it.

This was a big development. Lately he'd taken to stroking Fred and whispering something in the parrot's ear. Once or twice she'd caught him with Fred, looking guilty—and she was sure he'd been talking to the bird. But now Perran felt safe enough to make a sound or two in front of them.

Laura quickly dressed Kerenza and cuddled the little girl, giggling at Max and Perran's silly antics, inwardly tense because the sooner her nephew talked, the sooner she would have to leave. And yet she longed for him to chatter.

'Breakfast, guys,' she said decisively. 'Anyone not down by the time I've counted twenty will be eating their knickers.'

With roars of horror, Max and Perran pushed her aside and thundered down the stairs, turning into aeroplanes on the way, by the sound of it.

Shaken by the sudden development, she followed more sedately.

'I thought Tintagel,' she said, when the bacon and eggs had been dished up.

Max looked up from supervising Kerenza's bottle.

'Been there, Perran?' The little boy shook his head. 'King Arthur's castle,' Max said enthusiastically. 'Where he lived long ago, with beautiful ladies in long dresses and men in armour and swords. Gosh, this is difficult explaining!' He appealed to Laura.

'There was a wizard,' she said, in tones of hushed awe. Perran's eyes rounded. 'We'll show you his cave where he did his magic.'

'O-o-h!' squealed Perran.

Somehow she and Max refrained from leaping up and shouting, 'Y-e-s!' They both kept their eyes down on their plates.

'Not long now, I think,' Max said quietly.

Her throat clogged with tears. 'No.'

He took her hand, kissed it and smiled at her bewildered face. 'Hang on in there. We'll make it.'

'Uh-huh.'

All that day, they were 'the family' again. Perran adored the tourist shops, with their wizards' hats, mock swords, medieval armour and King Arthur colouring books. But he surprised them by choosing a piece of quartz crystal as the present they'd promised him, and he held it in his hand throughout the long walk down to the castle, stealing excited, reverent looks at it and quite touching Laura's heart.

'Wow!'

She stiffened, then pulled herself together. 'Fantastic, isn't it, Perran?' she said eagerly.

He stared at the vertiginous steps leading up to the castle dramatically set on the edge of the cliff and nodded, apparently unaware he'd spoken at all.

Max slid out of the baby-carrier and lifted Kerenza out. 'Let's have a picture,' he said. 'Special moment.'

Before she could say anything, he'd approached a stranger, and she realised with growing dismay that he meant a family snap. 'No, Max, I'll take it!' she cried sharply.

'All of us.' He flashed her such a hard, uncompromising look that she quailed. 'Perran would like it,' he growled. 'Don't be so damn selfish!'

'Oh. Yes. I—I hadn't thought.'

She lined up where Max directed, the castle behind them, the sea crashing against the cliffs in flurries of white spray. She clutched Kerenza, a frozen smile on her face. Perran stood proudly in front of Max, grinning happily and holding his treasured crystal aloft.

Her heart lurched. The camera would lie.

'Smile!' ordered Max under his breath as the stranger brought the camera to his eye. 'Not that glacial snarl!'

Hurt, she said, 'Cheese,' for Perran's sake. One day he'd look at the photo and think of the happy times they'd had. He would never know her heart had been breaking, she thought forlornly.

'Thanks very much,' Max said warmly to the stranger.

'No problem. Not often you get the whole family together, is it? Photos like these are precious, I know. See you around.'

'Yes.'

She glanced at Max. He was clearing his throat, his face grim as he took Kerenza from her and settled the sleepy little girl in the baby-carrier again.

'It was a lovely thought,' she said shakily. 'We must take several pictures today and get them developed. Perhaps buy a frame so Perran—'

But he'd stomped off in a temper for some reason, slipping the carrier on his back and catching Perran's hand, striding so fast that the boy had to run as fast as his little legs would carry him to keep up.

She followed, wondering what she'd said. Slowly she climbed the steep steps, not even worrying about the drop to the sea on either side as she usually had whenever she'd come before.

They met up again on the highest point. Without a word, he handed the carrier to her and went off with Perran to play knights, a game which involved a lot of pretend sword fighting and clashing sounds as the 'swords' supposedly met.

The stranger joined in, with his family of three boys, and they were all causing much amusement with their blood-curdling cries.

Laura watched Perran having the time of his life. Heard him imitating the others. Full of love for him, she sat on the grass, intent on preserving this moment so that she could remember it in the future.

'Load of kids, all of them, aren't they?' said a young woman, flinging herself to the ground beside her. But she smiled affectionately at the two men as they fooled around, and Laura realised this must be the stranger's wife. 'Still. Wouldn't be without them, would we?'

Laura managed a smile and made some kind of stumbling reply.

She had a short time left. She would remember her mother's advice: live every moment.

'Excuse me,' she said with a friendly smile to the woman, 'I think they need a damsel in distress.'

Nearing them, she saw Max stop and falter, take a fatal sword blow to the heart, and drop to his knees. But he kept on watching her, his eyes fixed on her flushed face and huge eyes.

'Rescue me!' she cried, wringing her hands. 'The wicked knight has cast a spell on me and the baby princess! His magic is forcing me down to the beach...'

With a whoop of joy, Perran started slashing at imaginary foes. She turned and made her way down, wondering briefly if she should be encouraging sword fights, however benign. But when she saw Perran's happy face, and Max's grateful one, she knew it didn't matter.

After she had been saved by a mixture of magic shells and seaweed arranged in a mystic circle on the sands of Tintagel Haven, they found a place near the waterfall for their picnic and sat enjoying the weak October sun and the wildness of the scene.

She knew there was no substance in the legend of King Arthur and that the castle had probably belonged to a Cornish chieftain. But, like thousands of others, she wanted to believe in it.

And she was prepared to play make-believe with Max right up to the hilt, she thought, with a smile at the aptness of that.

'I'm coping with this,' she said quietly to Max, when Perran had trotted off to find dragons. 'I love him so much.' She gave a light laugh. 'Divorced couples act civilly in front of their children if they care for them more than their own petty differences. I don't think I'll have any difficulty.'

'Fine.'

She touched his arm, unhappy with his curtness. 'Please, Max—'

'Time I was a dragon, I think.' He rose stiffly and strode away.

Disappointed, she gave up, and spent the rest of the afternoon having as much fun as possible, taking a whole reel of pictures so that she could preserve this day for ever.

There was a noticeable tension about Max that evening. She kept her nose in her book, boning up on insects. He zapped through the channels on the television, then lapsed into silence. She knew he was watching her, brooding about something, but she refused to look up.

'I'm going to bed,' he announced, walking out before she could even acknowledge his remark.

It was only ten o'clock. Laura did her best to study, but it was very difficult. Her thoughts kept straying to Max and the children. She went into the kitchen to make herself a hot drink, and suddenly stopped. Max was pacing up and down in the bedroom overhead, fast, short, impatient strides, as though he was angry about something.

She stayed up for another hour and then couldn't put off going to bed any longer. She checked the children. Perran was still clutching his treasured crystal. Smiling gently, she kissed him and Kerenza.

When she reached their bedroom door, she saw that Max was asleep. Relieved, she tiptoed about and cautiously crept under the duvet, sliding in inch by inch, petrified of disturbing him.

He rolled over, muttering in his sleep, and she held her breath as his arm drew her close. She sighed and gave herself to the pleasure of being in his arms, watching his beautiful, blissful face, the appealingly softened mouth.

I love you, she said to him silently, and snuggled contentedly against him, drifting off to sleep.

Dreams filled her head—so real that she could feel every sensation. Max's hand moving over her back. His breath on her face. Warmth invading the recesses of her body. Max touching her tenderly, kissing her forehead, her mouth, her jawline...

And then she realised that this was real. Knowing she should stop him, she feigned sleep and gave herself totally to the illicit love-making.

This was the gentlest of seductions. Max seemed hardly awake—perhaps he wasn't. He seemed to want to kiss and kiss her, sweetly, delicately, as though she were as fragile as the crystal jug which she had shattered. She lay for an eternity, not daring to make a sound, letting him have free access to her singing body, and the sweetness of his loving made it all the harder to bear.

His mouth began to wander. Each inch of skin was given his entire attention, and was left bereft when he moved on. Laura was being driven mad. When his lips finally nuzzled at her breast and his hand found the hot liquidness between her thighs, she let out a sudden, involuntary groan.

And he stopped, frozen, as if he'd woken.

Her love-drugged eyes opened. He was looking at her in shock, the whites of his eyes wide and gleaming in the darkness.

Then they narrowed, and he was storming out of the room.

'Max!' She dashed after him, slid on a rug and ended up crashing to the floor, whimpering with pain.

He switched on the overhead light and flooded the room with brightness. 'Oh, God! Laura!'

'I—I can't help f-falling!' she sobbed. 'Ouch!'

'Sorry.' Scowling ferociously, he sat back on his haunches with an expression of utter defeat, smoothing back his hair as if he was still dazed with sleep. 'Where does it hurt?' he asked politely, wearily.

'My back. But I'll be all right. I'm winded and a bit bruised.'

'I'll get the arnica—'

'No!' She didn't want him rubbing anything on her back. 'Give me your hand and help me up. There. See? I'm fine.'

'Try walking.'

She did. 'I can. Max... About...just now... I'm sorry. I was asleep—'

'Yeah.'

Her lip trembled. 'What are you going to do? Where are you going?' she asked, rubbing her sore back.

'Somewhere. Anywhere.'

He suddenly noticed his nakedness. And that he was highly aroused. Two high spots of colour touched his cheekbones, and he turned his back to her. Striding angrily to the wardrobe, he pulled out various items of clothing. Too many to wear all at once. His intention became clear when he lifted out two pairs of shoes.

'You can't go away!' she cried, white with dismay.

'I am.' He dragged down his boot bag and started stuffing items into it. 'Marrakesh. We've got to get Fay and Daniel back.'

'It's...the middle of the night!'

'The roads'll be clear.'

'You haven't a flight—'

'I'll wait for one!'

'Perran—'

'Carry on the good work. Tell him I had to go to see his mummy and daddy, and give him my love. You know the kind of thing.'

'But—'

'No. I've had enough of your "buts",' he growled. 'I can't stop touching you and it's crucifying me, Laura! So you'll have to cope here. I'm off.'

'Oh, please, Max! I need you here. The children need you. We had a great time today, didn't we? And he's close to speaking—I want you to be around when he does.'

'I have to go,' he said irritably. 'I don't want to end up doing something I regret.'

'Like...what?' she asked, suddenly tense.

His face twisted. 'Laughing too much. Having too good a time. Loving too much,' he muttered savagely.

She longed to embrace him, to soothe away that look of anguish and tell him the truth. He loved her, and she wasn't strong enough to keep denying her love for him in this way.

'I'm—'

'Sorry?' he snapped. 'Too damn late for that! Don't stop me. Let me leave. At least allow me a dignified exit.'

She knew he was at the end of his tether. Her hands fluttered in resignation. He packed his bag in a stony silence and then he took a step towards the door. Laura ran to him.

'Ring me!' she begged hoarsely, clutching at his arm.

He shook her hand off as if it were something contagious. 'I'll call at five each day, GMT, so Perran can speak to me,' he clipped out.

'How long will you be?'

'As long as it takes. There's money in my wallet. Use it. You'll need taxis to do the shopping. Spend what you like.'

She stared at him numbly. He left the room without even a backward glance or a goodbye. When she heard the front door slam, the car engine start up and the crunch on the gravel, she ran to the window and snatched back the curtains.

The tail lights glowed at the entrance. And then he was gone.

CHAPTER NINE

'PERRAN! Max is coming home today!' Laura dumped the telephone receiver down and opened her arms to Perran, spinning around in excitement. 'Two weeks!' she complained. 'How could he stay away from us for so long? Hey!' she spluttered. 'You're choking me! Come on. We'd better make his favourite chocolate cake. And then we'll all get poshed up and smelling lovely. He's at the airport, he said. It'll take him hours to drive back. Plenty of time to get the house tidied. What a mess we've left it in!'

She paused for a comment, an 'mmm' even. Nothing. Not a sound—other than laughter and giggles—since Max had gone. He was an important part of Perran's progress towards speech. An important part of her life too, she thought wistfully.

'Pinnies on!' She whirled into the kitchen where Kerenza was safely ensconced, chuckling at the mobile over her playpen. Laura set the oven then snapped on the radio and jigged about to the music.

'Chop-chop! Flour! Butter! Eggs!' She rapped out orders in mock authority and Perran scuttled about with a happy smile on his face, and she—she wanted to...

'Dance with me!' she cried to Perran, catching him and the cake tin he was carrying and sweeping both into her arms.

Max was coming home!

She stopped in mid-twirl. Managed a grin for Perran and plonked him on a chair so that he could help. Weighed the flour. Began to tremble.

How long had they got? He'd been cagey, refusing to

say anything till he returned. She whizzed up the eggs and butter. The news hadn't been good about Fay, but maybe he'd got her off. If he was bringing Fay back, then...

'Tip the flour and cocoa in, darling,' she said brightly. 'Switch on.'

They watched the mixture combining. This day would be the best they'd ever had, she vowed. The happiest. No thought of tomorrow.

She and Perran took spoons, when the cake was cooking, and dived into the mixing bowl, scraping up the last remnants of the chocolate mixture. Flushed with cooking, Laura was chatting happily all the time, pushing back her falling hair, not caring where flour or cake mix went, intent only on being happy.

'Shall we dance again, with Kerenza?' she asked, filled with a frenetic madness.

Without waiting for a reply, she lifted up the baby and swirled about the kitchen, ignoring the cooking chaos and the jumble of books and rulers in the drawing room, where she and Perran had done their showjumping practice. Kerenza had squealed in delight to see the two of them neighing and tossing their manes, completing clear rounds every time.

Laura laughed at herself for being so daft. 'Oh, my darling, darling Perran,' she cried in tearful affection as he tried to skip, like her. 'I love you to pieces!'

Bright-eyed, the little boy wrapped his arms about her knees and squeezed, his face uplifted and adoring.

'Having a lovely time?' she asked tenderly. He nodded, and she smiled. 'It'll be perfect when Max comes home, won't it?'

There was a movement to her left, and she twisted her head around, dumbfounded to see Max there, watching them.

He came forward, bent down, tapped the unsuspecting

Perran on the shoulder and laughingly suffered a near neck strangulation as a result.

'You—you said you were at the airport! Heathrow's several hundred miles away!' she cried, ridiculously, joyously pleased to see him.

'Newquay,' he explained, referring to a nearby small airport. 'I drove there, left my car and flew up to London from there two weeks ago. Came back that way too. Everything been all right?'

'Wonderful. How's...?'

'Tell you later. We need to be alone.' He smiled at her. 'I'm looking forward to the chocolate cake.'

'How did you know I'd done one?'

He laughed. 'Your face, hair, everywhere! Have you looked in the mirror lately?'

'Oh!' She brushed a hand over her face and encountered sticky chocolate around her mouth. Which curved in amusement. 'Am I as mucky as Perran?' she asked, her eyes twinkling.

'Worse.' He looked around, one eyebrow raised.

'We were going to tidy,' she said quickly. 'One big clean. And the drawing room's OK, really; it's just that we were showjumping and—'

'I'm not criticising. Far from it. It's lovely to be back.'

He seemed content just to look at her. She waited for him to go on, but he was studying her as if he'd never seen her before.

'Have I developed a squint or something? Spots? Turned yellow?' she asked, her breath catching in her throat.

'Radiance.' Oblivious of her astonishment, he pulled out a chair and let Perran snuggle up on his lap.

'Bottom!' screamed Fred suddenly, from his perch in the far corner.

Perran dissolved into giggles and burrowed deeper. Max and Laura gaped at one another, and then at the minute bit of Perran's head which was showing from underneath Max's jacket. She and Max began to laugh, and soon she was clutching weakly at the kitchen table.

Fred danced up and down. 'Bottom! Bottom! Bottom!'

Perran seemed to be a mass of shaking stripes. He was wearing his favourite shirt again.

'Well!' marvelled Max. 'I didn't know Fred could talk!'

'Neither did I!' chuckled Laura. 'He's never said a word before.'

'And what a word to choose!' Max grinned at her.

'Rather naughty,' she agreed. Her face was alight with love and pleasure. 'How clever of him to speak, though,' she said gently.

'Wonderful.' Max looked at her with a mixture of pleasure and pain.

Perran was close to speaking. She turned away, unable to meet his eyes any longer. 'Well,' she said, feigning brightness. 'Let's tell Max what we've been doing. What do you say, Perran? Shall we tell him?'

He didn't answer, though his scarlet face emerged from its hiding place and he looked at Laura expectantly.

She started ticking off their activities. 'We saw where the fish were caught, and the lobster cages. We went out on a boat—just in Port Isaac bay—and we had ice creams, and a seagull came down and pinched Perran's. We bought a kite and flew it on the Main, we fed the cows grass—'

'What?' Max's eyes were laughing at her.

'They had grass, but we found them longer, better stuff. They liked it a lot,' she defended. 'We bought a piskie for luck and threw coins in the wishing well, and we've done loads of gardening and Perran knows the names of all the insects we found—'

'You're wonderful, Laura. You know that?'

Her eyes flickered with anxiety and then became unnaturally bright. 'Fantastic,' she agreed in a brittle voice. 'Perfect, that's me.'

'No. I'm not teasing. I mean it.'

'Max, you promised!' she said chokily, and stomped out.

A little while later, without flour and chocolate mix in every conceivable place, she stalked into the kitchen to check the cake.

A brief glance at Max revealed him to be holding both Kerenza and Perran in his arms, all three of them nearly asleep, pink and glowing in the warmth from the boiler and the oven.

Very quietly, she opened the glass door and tested the cake. Done. She lifted it out to cool on the rack, and turned.

'They're well away.' Max was putting the children down, the baby in her little buggy, Perran in the armchair. The little boy's arm flopped out loosely, and Max's face was so loving that Laura's heart all but stopped. 'I need to talk to you about Fay. Let's sit on the terrace. It's lovely out there.'

Laura followed him out, her pulses racing, afraid that her sister might be in trouble, afraid that Max would want her to stay another week or more, afraid that she'd have to go. Muddled? Her? she thought wryly.

'Don't close the door,' she said, when Max pulled it shut behind him. 'We'll want to hear the children.'

'Laura,' he said gently, 'I think it would be better if the door was shut. Sit down.'

Keyed up, she sat, her eyes large with dread. 'There's something wrong, isn't there?'

'I'm afraid so.'

She bit her lip, and Max took both her hands comfortingly in his. 'Tell me.'

'I've failed,' he said simply.

Laura let out a little cry. 'They—they've been found guilty?'

'Fay confessed.' He frowned. 'I don't think she had much option. She told me that...' His frown became a scowl and he wouldn't look at Laura any more. 'Daniel is an addict,' he said starkly. 'What started as a bit of fun, a means of getting high and spaced out, became a terrible need. Daniel's going through hell from withdrawal symptoms. Fay's blaming everyone but herself.'

She was stunned. And Max...he'd been through hell too. 'I'm so sorry,' she said softly. 'It must have hurt you desperately to see him.'

His mouth shaped into a grimace. 'Foul,' he agreed in a low tone, still staring at their entwined hands. 'But as I came nearer and nearer to you and the children I felt my depression lifting. I walked in and found you...' His lashes lifted. She quivered at the misty look of tenderness and love. Quivered and ached. 'I found you,' he went on in a hoarse whisper, 'looking so beautiful, like a madonna. So *loving*. And I confess that I forgot Fay and Daniel for a moment or two because you did my heart good. Your sister has ruined more than her own life. But you, you, my darling,' he said, moving closer, 'make up for all the evil she's strewn around.'

'Oh, Max!' she cried jerkily, snatching her hand away and jumping up in agitation. 'I've told you—'

'I know.' He came to stand behind her and put his arms around her so that she was his prisoner. And she had no idea if she was willing or not. 'Trouble is,' he said, 'your mouth says one thing and everything else says another.'

'Perhaps,' she snapped, dipping down and slipping from his arms and moving away, 'I'm just sex-mad.'

'I'm talking about love.'

'And I want to know about my sister!' she cried, spinning round to face him. 'What's going to happen to her?'

'OK, OK!' He put up his hands in a conciliatory gesture. 'One thing at a time. Fay first, because her future has a bearing on ours.'

'Not ours,' Laura said miserably. 'We are not and never will be an *item*! Stop being so dense, Max!'

'We're being forced together. Fay's lawyer says she's likely to get between fifteen and twenty years.'

'Fif...!' Her voice disintegrated. Slowly her legs gave way too, and she staggered to the bench. Fifteen years. For someone so lively, bubbly... 'Oh, God!' she groaned, covering her face with her hands.

He held her, stroking, soothing. 'All right, love. Gently.'

'It's terrible, Max!' she said, lifting her ashen face. 'The most awful thing to happen. And what about Daniel?'

'His future is uncertain. But I think it'll be a similar sentence.'

For a while she sat immobile, trying to come to terms with her sister's fate. 'Poor Fay,' she said miserably. And then her head jerked up. 'The...the children!' she cried, grabbing Max urgently. 'What about them? Who's...?'

He was waiting for the penny to drop, and it dropped. Max expected her to care for them. Perhaps with him. Acting like husband and wife but never being husband and wife.

Or perhaps he'd use her for sex, since both of them seemed incapable of restraint. Or perhaps he expected them to marry, to have children—yes. Of course. Max loved children so much that he'd want his own; she'd already worked that out. Why was her brain being so slow?

'You need a moment to think about this,' he said gently. 'I'll go and check on them, and we'll take this further.'

She stood there, shaking, not wanting anyone or anything to go anywhere. She wanted time to go backwards, to the days when she and Max had been sleeping together, making love, happy and oblivious to the problems to come.

And then she heard him shouting, and although she couldn't hear clearly for a moment something in his tone made her blood run cold.

'What, Max?' she yelled, racing into the house.

He came out as if devils were after him. 'They're not there!'

Her mouth opened. No sound came out.

'The children! They've both gone!' He caught her arm and shook her. 'I'll search the house from top to bottom,' he rapped. 'You check the car's still there; look around the garden. Go! Hurry!'

Stumbling, gasping in fear, she raced to the garage. One car.

'Perran!' she screamed.

No answer. Sobbing, calling his name, she scanned the far hill which led out of Port Gaverne for any sign of a car whisking the children away to God knew what fate. Nothing.

'Perran!'

A sound. She controlled her sobs, held her breath. A child, somewhere in the garden, shouting hysterically.

'Let him be all right! Oh, please, let him not be hurt!' she sobbed, running headlong towards the sound.

The field. The cattle... Laura blanched. At the far end of the field the cattle were grouped together, pushing towards something...

'*Perran!*' she screamed, and vaulted the high fence without a thought, running harder than she'd ever run in her life. The cattle had seen her. They'd turned and were thundering towards her. Not caring, her eyes fixed only on that tiny, furious figure in the yellow and black striped top, she hurtled on, praying she didn't trip over in the hoof-rutted field—because if she did, she'd go under the oncoming herd and be no use to Perran...

Miraculously she was through them. 'Here I am!' she

cried, yards away from where he was fiercely brandishing a stick, Kerenza screaming in her buggy behind his sturdy little back.

She scooped him up, dropped him anyhow on the other side of the fence—barbed wire here. Unsnapping Kerenza's harness, she held her over the fence, ripping her jumper on the barbs as she did so.

'Take her from me, darling,' she said, trying to sound calm. 'Are you strong enough? Good boy! Put her on the ground very gently. I'm coming over.'

How? The cattle were regrouping, trotting back to investigate. Heifers weren't dangerous, but they were curious—and there was always a chance that one would barge into the other and stumble, knock her to the ground and...

Laura took off her jumper and laid it across the barbed wire, then did a kind of roll over it. For a moment she hung in mid-air as the barbs went through jumper, shirt, skin, and then she was free. Hurting, bleeding, but free.

'Well!' she said brightly, checking that Kerenza was unharmed and holding her to her breast in relief. 'That was exciting, wasn't it?'

'They made baby cry,' Perran told her warily, so evidently worried she'd be angry that she gave him a kiss. 'I got a stick. I waved it at them,' he went on proudly. 'I saved baby.'

'Oh, darling, you were so brave,' she said, deeply touched by his protective instincts. 'But why were you there?'

'I took her for a walk. To be like Max. I want to be Max when I grow up.'

She looked at him helplessly. And then realised. Perran was talking. Tears sprang to her eyes and she brushed them away furiously.

'He's looking for you,' she said shakily. 'We'd better get back and let him know you're all right.'

The field was overgrown with brambles and hawthorn.

They broke branches off small trees and hacked a way clear. Progress was slow, and she was conscious of the fact that Max would be out of his mind with worry.

She saw him, leaning out of a window, presumably searching for her. 'Hey!' she yelled. 'We're here; we're all right!'

His head went in and in a few moments he was racing towards them, and then he had gathered them, Laura and all, into his big embrace. They stayed like that for a few moments, then Max broke away and he and Laura looked a little embarrassed.

'What happened?' he asked, breathing heavily. 'Where were they? What——?'

'Tell him, Perran.'

'Lorra was brave,' he declared, full of admiration.

Max's mouth dropped open when Perran spoke. He looked at Laura and she nodded, her face solemn. His mouth tightened and his expression had the same mixture of pain and delight as hers must have had.

Perran was talking. Happiness and sorrow intermingled.

'Was she?' Max muttered hoarsely.

'She ran all through the cows. I love Lorra.'

'My God!' said Max faintly. 'You...ran through a herd of heifers? You idiot!' he yelled, more angrily than he needed. 'You could have been killed! One stumble and they'd have been smashing your head——'

'Hush!' She telegraphed alarm, her eyes indicating that Perran would be distressed. But she felt cherished. Loved. And she knew why he'd lost his cool. She felt tense too.

Max subsided. She noticed his hand was shaking when it closed around hers. 'I think,' he said, 'a little talk about going off without permission is in order. After that, everything else is on hold till a certain someone is in bed.'

* * *

Why she put on her—and Max's—favourite dress that night, she didn't know. Or why she took an inordinate time to do her face and hair.

Perhaps, she thought, staring back at her reflection, because this was showdown time. She had to tell Max he had to bring the children up without her. And if she was leaving in the morning, because she wouldn't be capable of staying in the same house with him, then she'd go out in style.

To avoid talking about Perran—and what it meant now that he had found his voice—she asked him about the past two weeks in Marrakesh.

Over dinner he described what a nightmare it had been, how helpless he'd felt. All the time she kept wanting to take him in her arms and hold him close.

She made a mess of getting coffee. Half the packet spilled all over the counter-top. Then she discovered she hadn't put any water in the espresso machine. Then she forgot to switch it on.

At last she was carrying the tray in, past Max, who'd been standing in the kitchen watching her intently, making her nervous, making no comment or even bothering to tell her the things she'd forgotten.

The tray wobbled as she carried it through to the drawing room, followed closely by Max. A cup slid; she must have been holding it at an angle. Laura fought to save it, but everything whizzed to one end and fell onto the expensive carpet.

She stared at the coffee stains, the spilled sugar, the smears of chocolate cake, drew in a huge, ragged breath and stalked back to start again.

'I'll do it.' Max pushed her away. 'Go and sit down.'

'I'll pay for the carpet.'

She slunk back and sat on the edge of a chair, eyeing the mess numbly. Now what would he remember of her? A clumsy, cack-handed woman who was absolutely use-less, who left the place in chaos and couldn't even manage to make coffee without making the kitchen look as if it had been the scene of World War III.

'The carpet,' said Max, when he brought a fresh tray in, 'can be cleaned. It's unimportant—'

'I'll pay for the cleaning, then.'

'Have a piece of cake.'

She looked at it longingly. 'I'll drop it everywhere.'

'Then bloody well drop it!' he cried in exasperation.

Laura blinked. 'Why are you angry with me?' she said unhappily.

'Because you're so unbelievably stupid.'

'Oh, thanks.' Miffed, she grabbed the plate and sank her teeth into the fluffy sponge.

'I want to tell you what Fay and Daniel have asked me to do.'

Laura felt her hand shaking and hastily put the cake down on the arm of her chair. 'Right.'

'I told them how we'd been looking after the children together. I reassured them that they were being well cared for.' He hesitated. Here it comes, she thought. You and me, mummies and daddies. Her stomach rolled with pain. 'They know what the score is,' he said quietly. 'Perran will be at least nineteen when Fay comes out.'

'No remission?' she asked, pale and dismayed.

'None.' Max sipped his coffee, watching her carefully as she digested the horror of that news.

'Poor Fay!' she whispered. 'Poor Daniel.'

He nodded. 'It's tough. I'm sorry. Laura...you know what I'm going to say. They want us to adopt the children.'

'No.'

There it was. Simple. She sat like a zombie, hands folded in her lap, legs together, feet neat. Only her brain was screaming. Only her stomach and her heart were clamouring for a different reply.

'Perran and Kerenza need the two of us, Laura,' he said, his eyes never leaving her face. 'You know that.'

'Better you with the help of a nanny who doesn't drop coffee, who doesn't smash jugs—'

'Who doesn't play showjumping and dance about and who doesn't love the children with all her heart... Oh, Laura!' he said fondly. 'Don't you see what you can offer them?'

'And what do I offer you?' she muttered obstinately.

'You're everything to me. I've told you this before. You light up my life. I want to live with you for ever—'

'Nothing's for ever!' she cried, jerking her arms in a defensive gesture. The plate clattered to the floor, the cake landing icing side down. 'Oh, *damn*! I don't believe it!' she raged. And then snapped her head around to glare at Max.

He was laughing. Throwing his beautiful head back and roaring with uncontainable laughter, tears of helpless amusement appearing on his cheeks.

'I do love you, sweetheart!' he said fondly.

'Glad I'm so darn funny!' she sobbed.

He was with her in seconds, his arms holding her tightly. 'Now, listen,' he said sternly. 'You have to marry me because you love me. We're happy together. You love the children. Stop playing so hard to get—'

'I can't marry you!' she wailed, beating her hands against his chest in frustration. 'I can't! I want to, but I *can't*!'

He went very still. Pushed her back. Stared hard into her eyes in shock.

'You...' He swallowed. 'You're...married?' he asked hoarsely. 'An absent husband somewhere you haven't divorced?'

'No!'

A vast breath was eased from his lungs. He was trying to read her eyes, a new anxiety darkening his face. 'Darling...it's not a serious illness, is it?'

'No!' She had to say it. 'You want us to have children.'

'Of course!' He beamed. 'Loads. Brothers and sisters for Perran and... What is it? Is that the problem? Laura! Laura, speak to me!'

Her chin was being lifted. Miserably she met his eyes. And knew she had to hurt him.

'I can't have babies, Max.'

He started, studied her carefully, and slowly it dawned on him what she was saying. 'No...babies.' He rose from the arm of the chair and began walking round and round the coffee table as if in a daze.

She saw him thinking, working his way through all the situations of the past few weeks one by one. His demand that she look after Fay's children. Her daily contact with them. His declaration of love and her refusal. And now he was facing the end of *his* dream: fathering babies with her.

Finally he slumped in a chair. 'I can't believe what I've put you through,' he said, white-lipped.

She was taken aback. She'd been expecting him to be shattered because he wanted her to be a normal, healthy woman—and she wasn't. He hadn't recoiled from her. He wasn't angry because she'd ruined his plans.

'You want children of your own. You shouldn't be denied that,' she told him gently. 'You're rich. Gorgeous. There'll be plenty of women to choose from, who—'

'No. I want you.'

'But I can't—'

'It doesn't matter.' He came over and pulled her to her feet.

'It does! You'd resent me—'

'No. I'll love you. We have children. Perran and Kerenza. And you can go for special treatment, and who knows—?'

'No, Max.' So that was why he'd been so calm. Cold and composed, knowing she had to leave for his sake, she detached herself and put a yard or two between them. 'I can't have any treatment.'

'But...' His brow puckered in bewilderment. 'You mean...? There's no scar—'

'Modern operating techniques.' She wondered how she could be so unruffled, how long it would be before the strange stillness was peeled away and replaced by a sense of devastation. She was going to ask him to release her. To live separate lives. And that meant not seeing the children again.

Her eyes filled with tears.

'When did this happen?' he asked quietly.

She couldn't tell him. But her anguished eyes did that for her.

He froze, the horror suddenly draining his face of all colour. 'I made you pregnant!' A strangled, almost feral cry of protest was wrenched from his throat when she nodded dumbly. 'Why didn't you tell...?' His eyes closed. 'My parents. They invented that fiancée in Surrey. So you left for London. Pregnant and alone...'

'I had my aunt looking after me,' she reminded him.

'And...you lost the baby.'

'Fay—rang up—one day—when I was—five months,' she said in a series of little jerks.

'And that's when she told you about our so-called affair.' He stared at her, aghast. 'When she told you she was pregnant by me! God! If I'd known any of this, I wouldn't have bothered to try to bring her back from Marrakesh!'

'Yes, you would,' she said wearily. 'For Perran.'

'I don't know!' His fist crashed down on a nearby table, making her jump nervously. 'I don't know what the hell I think! Laura—' His voice had softened. With a tenderness in his eyes which stabbed her through and through, he held his arms out to comfort her.

'Sympathy's no good, Max,' she said, remaining ram-rod-stiff and fighting for control. 'None of this is your fault. We have to live with it. Best we don't ruin each other's lives. I'll sleep in the spare room. I want to stay till the morning so I can say goodbye to the ch-childr…' Tears stopped her from speaking. With a sob, she ran from the room.

Max didn't follow her. Forlornly she accepted that he'd finally acknowledged she had to go. That it was the wisest thing to do.

Laura buried her head in the pillow and cried herself to sleep. All alone. He really didn't love her for herself. All this time she'd been hoping he might. That he'd find out about her, and yet it wouldn't matter. But she couldn't blame him for wanting a real woman, a proper wife.

She woke late. Her face was a terrible sight, puffy and blotchy as it had been once before, the time they'd met again in her bedsit. Well, at least she was consistent, she thought, trying to cheer herself up and being totally unsuccessful.

The nursery was empty so Max had dealt with the children. Just as well, since he'd be doing that in future…

She bit back a sob. Breakfast, a cheery goodbye and off in a taxi.

Her hand touched something odd on the white-painted banister. Scarlet—*scarlet* icing sugar! As if someone had been…writing.

'Morning…' she read. She went down a few more steps. '…Laura.' She smiled feebly. A joke, for Perran. 'I love you.' Her brows met in a frown. She wasn't going to get away easily. 'Leave and…' The words continued—*on the wallpaper*! 'Max!' she breathed, shocked by his vandalism as she read on, '…I will never be happy. I'll teach you to drive…'

She had reached the kitchen door. All over it were lurid pink icing kisses. She could hear Perran giggling

behind it. Max shushing him. Taking a deep breath, she
flung the door open and reeled back.

The whole room was filled with cardboard balloons,
painstakingly cut out and coloured, string attached, fixed
to the ceiling so they looked as if they were floating.
Streamers made from newspapers looped from corner to
corner. Newspaper fringes adorned every possible ledge.
And everywhere she looked were icing declarations of
love, adoration, hearts...

Her astounded eyes scanned the two conspirators sitting at the table, their mouths ridiculously clamped together as they held back guilty laughter, their eyes wide
and watchful.

Only Kerenza was innocent, and she was wearing a
perky little paper hat with lipsticked hearts on it. Max
and Perran were wearing cereal packet crowns and foil
breastplates.

'Bottom! Bottom!' screeched Fred happily, making
Perran collapse into fits of giggles and fall off his chair.

'Oh, be quiet, you rude bird! You're ruining the effect!' Max muttered.

She smiled. At her feet was a plank of wood, whose
purpose she could only puzzle over.

'Drawbridge,' murmured Max, seeing her eyes goggle
at it.

'Of course,' she said faintly.

'You walk over it and pull it up.'

They stared at one another for a long time.

'Are you reading my eyes too?' he asked hopefully.

'I am!' she cried, hardly daring to believe what was
there.

He loved her. Unconditionally. And this was his mad
way of ensuring that she knew. Tidy, disciplined Max
had made the mother of all messes.

And suddenly Laura began to laugh with pure joy. All
at once Perran squealed in delight and clapped his hands.

'Here's your crown!' he cried, holding it up excitedly.

Her eyes adored Max. Carefully she walked across the plank and solemnly raised it up, wedging it against a chair. 'Now we're in our castle,' she said huskily.

'Are you cross about the mess?' asked Perran, awed.

'No. But that doesn't mean anyone can *ever* do anything like this again!'

'It'll wash off. Or I can repaint the woodwork,' said Max hastily. 'And we didn't like that wallpaper, did we?'

'No, we didn't,' she agreed with due solemnity.

'It took me all night,' Max said proudly.

She took the crown from Perran and went to Max. His arm came around her. 'I love you,' she said, trembling with emotion. 'You silly, wonderful idiot!'

'You're beautiful!' He drew her head down and kissed her tenderly.

'Nonsense! I look like Quasimodo on a bad day!' she protested.

But there were stars in his eyes. She could see them. 'Do you? You look stunning to me,' he sighed. 'That's love, isn't it?'

'You—you really don't mind about me?'

'I love you, not what you can do for me.' Max kissed her again. Perran began banging impatiently on the table with his fork. 'Kissing is part of being kings and queens,' he told Perran with dignity. 'We have to play the game.'

'Soppy,' muttered Perran, and began tucking into a sausage.

Laura and Max looked at one another and burst out laughing. 'What have we let ourselves in for?' she said with a pretend groan.

'Bottom!' muttered Fred, giving them the hint of an idea.

She giggled and stroked Max's hair. 'You were saying?'

'That it doesn't matter to me what you are, what you

do, whether we can have children or not. It was a shock, yes. I had plans, I admit. But they're not the most important thing for me. Only the fact that you'll marry me.'

'Of course I will,' Laura said unsteadily. 'Oh! My mother will be *thrilled*! I must ring her!'

Despite Perran's groans, Max kissed her again. 'We can buy this house,' he told her, in between kisses. 'When I tell my parents what has happened they'll be in no position to refuse after what they've done.'

'It would be wonderful to live here, Max!' she said, her eyes shining. 'You know how much I love it here. We can get Perran a r-a-b-b-i-t and a—'

'Yes,' Max said quickly. 'Other animals. Don't waste precious time spelling everything!'

She couldn't keep the silly smile off her face. 'I can help in the local animal shelter...'

'And I can work from anywhere,' he murmured. 'I want nothing more but to live with you.'

'And the children.'

His eyes softened. 'And them.'

'And Fred.'

'Ah. I knew there was a catch somewhere.' Max grinned. 'He loathes me!'

Laura laughed, and kissed him tenderly. 'You can't win them all!' she murmured. 'Now, about that white meringue and the elephant you promised me...'

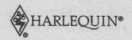
HARLEQUIN®

Not The Same Old Story!

Exciting, glamorous romance stories that take readers around the world.

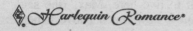

Sparkling, fresh and tender love stories that bring you pure romance.

Bold and adventurous—Temptation is strong women, bad boys, great sex!

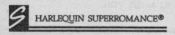

Provocative and realistic stories that celebrate life and love.

Contemporary fairy tales—where anything is possible and where dreams come true.

Heart-stopping, suspenseful adventures that combine the best of romance and mystery.

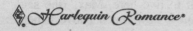

Humorous and romantic stories that capture the lighter side of love.

Take 2 bestselling love stories FREE

Plus get a FREE surprise gift!

Special Limited-Time Offer

Mail to Harlequin Reader Service®

3010 Walden Avenue
P.O. Box 1867
Buffalo, N.Y. 14240-1867

YES! Please send me 2 free Harlequin Presents® novels and my free surprise gift. Then send me 6 brand-new novels every month, which I will receive months before they appear in bookstores. Bill me at the low price of $3.12 each plus 25¢ delivery and applicable sales tax, if any*. That's the complete price, and a saving of over 10% off the cover prices—quite a bargain! I understand that accepting the books and gift places me under no obligation ever to buy any books. I can always return a shipment and cancel at any time. Even if I never buy another book from Harlequin, the 2 free books and the surprise gift are mine to keep forever.

106 HEN CH69

Name	(PLEASE PRINT)	
Address	Apt. No.	
City	State	Zip

This offer is limited to one order per household and not valid to present Harlequin Presents® subscribers. *Terms and prices are subject to change without notice. Sales tax applicable in N.Y.

UPRES-98   ©1990 Harlequin Enterprises Limited